Writer in Residence: A Novel

Paul Combs

The Stratford Press
USA

ALSO BY PAUL COMBS

The Last Word

Writer in Residence: A Novel

Copyright © 2015 by Paul Combs. All rights reserved.

Printed in the United States of America

ISBN-13: 978-0692496572
ISBN-10: 0692496572

Published by The Stratford Press

10 9 8 7 6 5 4 3 2 1

First Edition

For my girls

"Well, you know when people are no good at anything else they become writers." – W. Somerset Maugham, *The Razor's Edge*

1

"The Church of The Last Word"

The antique street lamps along Houston Street cast an eerie glow filtered through the rain that arrived after closing time, thumping against the tinted-glass display windows at the front of the shop. The light, however, illuminates nothing and the rain drenches no one; the streets are empty. Inside the shop, Sal Terranova leans back against the front checkout counter. The receiver of an ancient rotary phone rests on his shoulder, an unlit cigarette dangling absently from his lips.

"Yes, sir," he says into the phone, "I'm quite familiar with the book. It is, after all, a classic." He pauses while the person on the other end of the phone speaks.

"Yes, I understand that we say we can find any book for any customer." The store motto is etched in the glass of the front window, after all. There is another long pause.

"Yes, sir, if you are willing to pay the price it's typically not that difficult to find a signed Hemingway." There's a longer pause while the caller speaks more loudly.

"Again, I'm sorry to say there simply are no signed copies of *A Moveable Feast* available anywhere." This time the pause is much shorter.

"Because it was published three years after Hemingway died." Long pause.

"Yes, sir, I'm quite certain." After yet another pause, Sal gently places the telephone receiver back in its cradle. The caller has hung up.

Sal laughs out loud in the empty store as he turns to watch the rain outside grow heavier. A signed copy of *A Moveable Feast*. It was a crazy request, of course, but then he had seen more than a few crazy things since he went from burglar to bookseller.

Camden Templeton and Heather Morrison are returning from a late lunch. They are in no hurry, as the weather is perfect and being in the sun definitely beats being inside. As they reach the bookstore, however, they find several irritated customers standing outside the store, unable to enter, their way blocked by two large wooden shipping crates. Three burly delivery men in grimy coveralls are attempting, with no success, to move the crates inside. Just inside the door, nearly obscured by the crates, is Sal Terranova, shouting instructions.

"We're gonna have to take them out of the crates" he says. "But be very careful."

One of the men hurries to a nearby truck and returns with a crowbar. As he pries away at the crate, Camden pushes her way through the growing crowd and up to the door. Sal sees her and gives a thumbs-up sign.

"What in the bloody hell is all this, Terranova?" she demands, causing the man with the crowbar to take a wary step back.

He glances from her to the workman, who is just visible to him around the edge of the crate. He does not like her tone.

"Keep working on that crate," he says to the man. "Hang on, Cam. I'm coming out." He disappears from view, apparently taking the fire exit that leads into the alley behind the shop. In less than two minutes he is standing beside her. The man still hasn't made any progress on the crate.

"Somebody was serious when they packed this fucker," he says, then immediately follows with a "sorry, ma'am" to Camden. She gives him a curt smile and turns quickly to Sal.

"Why are there two large crates preventing our customers from entering our bookstore?" she asks through gritted teeth.

"Taxes," Sal replies.

For a second she is not sure she heard him right. Of the innumerable answers he could have given, "taxes" never even crossed her mind.

"What?" she asks.

"Taxes," he repeats, smiling now. "I have found a way to significantly reduce our taxes."

"What is in those crates, Sal?"

"Saints, my dear cousin," he says. "Saints."

This is an even stranger answer than "taxes." Clearly Sal is hell-bent on infuriating her. She looks to Heather for support, but Heather is laughing too hard to be of any help.

"What does 'saints' mean, exactly?" she asks as calmly as she can manage. There are customers, or would-be customers at any rate, watching.

"I will explain everything after we get these boxes opened," he says. "Why don't you take these nice people into the store through the back entrance?" He turns to the small crowd of people. "We have a treat for you today folks," he says in a carnival barker voice. "You are going to see the super-secret entrance to The Last Word Bookshop, a gateway through which few mortals ever pass. But you must keep what you see here a secret. Think of it as Bruce Wayne showing you the entrance to the Bat Cave."

This elicits several laughs, especially from two teenagers who regularly buy comic books from the store's small but carefully curated stock of them. Camden now has no choice but to do as Sal asked.

"This better be a bloody brilliant explanation," she growls at him, then leads the chattering group down the alley beside the store.

Camden cannot believe what she sees. The contents of the crates have been unloaded and now flank the checkout counter: two statues, each at least six feet tall, each standing on a stone pedestal. Chiseled into the stone of one are the words "St. John of the Cross," and on the other "St. Francis de Sales."

"Why are there statues of saints in my bookstore, Sal?" she asks.

"*Our* bookstore," he corrects her. "These two gentlemen belong here. Francis de Sales is the patron saint of writers, and John of the Cross is the patron saint of booksellers."

"You always said that Sylvia Beach was the patron saint of booksellers," Camden says, confused. "We even have her picture hanging over the counter."

"Her status is unofficial," Sal replies. "She was a Presbyterian, I think, so she can't legally be a saint."

"Legally? What are you talking about? What is this madness?"

"You gave me the idea, cousin," he says with a broad smile. "Remember a while back, how you were complaining that with the property taxes, school taxes, income taxes and every other kind of tax you were paying almost as much here as back in England?"

"Vaguely," she says with a suspicious glare.

"Well I found the answer. I am trying to have the store legally declared a place of worship. I call it the Church of The Last Word."

"The *what?*" she exclaims, then turns on Julia Hall, who is standing nearby trying her best not to laugh. "Did you know about this?"

"He might have mentioned it," Julia replies. "I didn't think he was serious. You know Sal and his ideas."

"Scoffing at my visionary plans will make for a lonely Valentine's Day for you, young lady," he says to Julia. She simply smiles and kisses him on the cheek.

"You cannot be serious," Camden says. She glances around and realizes that there are customers listening to this insane conversation. "Go to the back room, both of you," she says. "Now."

Sal seems hesitant to leave his new statues, but finally follows Camden and Julia to the space that serves as both break room and stock room. They sit at a small round table; Julia is still attempting not to laugh.

"A church," Camden says, her tone now more frustrated than angry. "What in the world are you thinking?

I hate paying taxes as much as anyone, but we are not a church."

"I disagree," Sal retorts. "In many ways that is exactly what we are: a place of refuge and inspiration and knowledge. Why not reap the benefits of that? And it's not that hard. For example, in order to meet the 'regular gathering together' clause, I started a Classics book club and reading group; we meet once a week."

"This so-called church cannot be recognized by the state as legitimate," Camden says.

"It's complicated, to be sure," Sal agrees. "But we are still officially under the umbrella of the Christian World Communion Church, even though we're technically a break-away congregation. My mother would be proud: I'm a schismatic. We're part of a class-action suit seeking official status, along with Jedi, Doctor Whovians, and Neo-Druids."

"The Christian World Communion Church?" Camden asks.

"It's a place that will ordain you online for ten dollars," Julia says. "Apparently he got 'ordained' years ago."

"But you're Catholic," Camden says.

"True, but back in Jersey I had friends who had been divorced and wanted to remarry. The Church won't do that, at least not without a lot of time and paperwork, so I handled it for them. Fifty bucks and all the beer and free food I wanted."

"But…" Camden began.

"And we're good on the incorporation aspect too," Sal continues without letting her protest further. "I set us up in Delaware, the state with the most lax incorporation laws in the country. So I'm ordained in California, the church is chartered in Texas, and we're incorporated in Delaware. Try following that rabbit trail."

"But can any of this insanity jeopardize the shop if you lose in court?" Camden asks, thinking this through to its logical, if horrifying, conclusion.

"Not the way I have it structured," he says, shaking his head. "Legally the shop itself is still an LLC owned by the two of us. We allow the church to use it for gatherings and such and count that as a donation to the church. The church is incorporated as a non-profit, and thus none of the salary we pay ourselves as clergy is taxable. Our salaries as owners are taxable, but we stop paying ourselves salaries as owners because we're already getting paid as clergy. You'll need to get ordained, by the way."

"This sounds like a Ponzi scheme," Julia says. She is not well versed on her con games.

"A Ponzi scheme would mean giving non-existent profits from a fake company or stock to investors using money from other investors and then blowing out the company or stock. None of that is happening here. This is strictly for tax avoidance…not evasion, avoidance. Besides, I always wanted my own belief system."

"Tell me again who your Pantheon is," Julia says.

"Homer, Shakespeare, Dante, Hemingway, and JK Rowling."

"I'm surprised Springsteen didn't make it in."

"I actually tried to make the whole thing about him...the Fellowship of the E Street Band. But the licensing fees and royalties he wanted in order for us to use his songs as our sacred text was just too exorbitant."

"And after you gave him that beautiful painting of him and the band as Jesus and the Apostles," Julia says with a grin. "But don't you have to pay fees to Rowling and Hemingway's estate? They're not in the public domain."

"We can read the books as part of the book club, we just can't print up any of it in our literature."

"We have literature?" Camden asks, alarmed.

"Well, not really. Just some flyers. For the most part the books themselves are our sacred texts."

"Jacob is going to have a coronary when he hears about this," Camden says. Jacob Weinberg manages the store's rare and collectible book section. He is a septuagenarian who worked for decade with Franklin Templeton, Sal and Camden's uncle, and grudgingly stayed on when they inherited the shop after Franklin's death.

"Jacob will be fine," Sal says. "The first book we're reading for the church group is Tolstoy's *The Kingdom of God is Within You.*"

"You're buying his support by starting with a Russian writer," Camden says, amazed.

"He does love his Russians," Sal says. "Ben won't care; he is probably already legally a Jedi himself. And Heather will be on board since Hemingway is one of our gods. He's been one of hers for years." Ben Williams handles the store's science fiction and fantasy section and the comic books, and Heather mainly manages literature.

"No, no, no," Camden says, beating her head on the table in time to her words. "This is not acceptable."

"Give it a chance, Cam," he says with a reassuring smile. "Everything's going to work out fine."

Things are slow the next day. Sunday afternoons are rarely busy until two or three o'clock; the store opens at 11:00, but people are at church or sleeping in and then at brunch or lunch after that. Sal, Jake Donovan, and Luis Ortiz stand in front of the statue of St. Francis de Sales, discussing Sal's plan.

Sal and Camden met Luis through one of their part-time employees, Ramon Sanchez, who is now a high school senior. Luis is a huge Puerto Rican with as shady a past as Sal. In fact, Luis's present was fairly shady, but that had not stopped Camden from going on several dates with him, much to everyone's surprise. Ortiz and Jake had been in the Army together, and he had introduced Jake to Sal and Camden.

"I think it is a grand idea, my friend," Ortiz says when Sal lays everything out for them. "I have been trying to get Jake to do something similar for years. The money we could make while saving the souls of poor and wretched sinners."

"I am not a televangelist, Lou," Jake says. "We have been over this a million times."

"I understand," Ortiz says with a sympathetic nod. "That is why I have always suggested that I handle the money side while you do the preaching. Everyone wins."

Out of the corner of his eye Jake sees Heather standing near a display table, organizing the current best sellers. He turns to looks at her, she turns at the same time, and their eyes meet. She winks, and he quickly looks away. She had flirted with him the last time he was in the shop, and though he was attracted to her raven hair, dark eyes, and love of literature…even her piercings and tattoos added to her allure, he thought…she was at least fifteen years younger than him, probably more. And his fiancé had been two aisles away.

"Jake," Ortiz says, "are you listening?"

Before he can answer the front door opens and Camden strides in, a small woman dressed all in black at her side. The three men stiffen immediately, and Sal recognizes the woman as a regular customer, one he tries his best to avoid. It is Sister Mary Louise, a nun from the convent attached to St. Joseph's Cathedral down the street. On their first meeting earlier that year she had shamed Sal into going to confession for the first time in a decade. She makes a beeline for the three of them, leaving Camden smiling in her wake.

"Salvatore Terranova," she says in a voice loud enough to be heard back in Jersey. "What is this blasphemy your sweet cousin is telling me about? Is it true that you are setting up false idols in this bookstore?"

Ortiz and Jake stare from the nun to Sal, nod a greeting at her, and hurry away. He is on his own with this one.

"These are not false idols, sister," Sal protests, not meeting her gaze. "They are honest to goodness saints."

"And used for purposes I am certain neither your dear mother nor our Lord himself would find appropriate. I can only imagine what St. Francis and St. John think of this wanton misuse if their holy likenesses."

"But sister," Sal says, gathering his courage. "I am still a Catholic. This is just a way to ease our tax burden. Surely the Lord wouldn't have a problem with that."

The words are barely out of his mouth before he realizes he has committed a fatal error; everyone standing nearby realizes it too. A verse from his catechism decades before appears in his mind, and as if by magic those very words leap from Sister Mary Louise's lips.

"You are to render unto Caesar what is Caesar's, Salvatore," she says with fire in her eyes. "Those are the words Jesus himself, and I do not think they leave any wiggle room, as you young people like to say."

Sal hangs his head, Camden beams triumphantly, and Julia simply shakes her head and smiles. She feels bad for Sal, but he really should have seen this coming.

"So," the nun continues, "I expect that before this end of the day, the Lord's Day if I need to remind you, that these statues will be removed and all of your diabolical plans rescinded."

"Diabolical?" Sal repeats. "That's a little harsh, sister."

"It means of the devil, and that's what this scheme of yours is. Harsh are the fires of Hell you will face if you don't change your ways. As it is I fear this will garner you a few million years in Purgatory."

Jake laughs out loud at this, for which he receives a withering glare from the nun. He stops laughing and stares down at his shoes.

"But what can I do with the statues, sister?" Sal asks. "The place I bought them from won't take them back."

"You can donate them to the cathedral," she says. "We always have room for more saints. You can come and implore their intercession when you have your next nefarious idea."

"That won't help me with the stained glass windows I ordered," he mutters.

"And why not?"

"The images are of Hemingway and Shakespeare and Dante," he says.

"I'll take the one of Hemingway," Heather shouts from across the room. The nun glares at her. "Sorry, sister," she says. "I'm a Wiccan; you don't scare me."

Sister Mary Louise regards her warily for a moment, then apparently decides this is a battle for another day. She turns back to Sal.

"And I have called Father Boyle," she tells him. "He usually doesn't hear confessions on Sunday, but given the extreme peril in which you have placed your soul, he will meet you at the church at 4:00 p.m."

Sal can imagine how much fun Father Boyle is going to have mocking him about this. Unlike the nun, he actually has a sense of humor. He drops all attempts at protest.

"Yes, sister," he says. "Let me get you a few Agatha Christie novels for the trouble of having to come down here to chastise me."

She nods, pleased that he has seen the error of his ways. As he leads her past a still-beaming Camden to the mystery section, Sal whisper to his cousin.

"You will pay for this, Templeton," he says. "If not in this life, then in the next."

2

"Three Guys Walk into a Bookstore"

Camden is happy. Tuesday is the day new books are released, and the store is filled with customers. A dozen red roses adorn the front counter, compliments of Ortiz, whom she is more and more starting to consider a boyfriend rather than just someone she's dating. Best of all, Sal is nowhere to be seen. It can't get much better than this, so of course it gets much, much worse.

As has often been her experience, her perfect day is shattered by the arrival of a man. Three men actually, almost simultaneously. The bell over the front door of the shop chimes, and in walks a broad-shouldered man in a cheap suit and dark glasses who can only be some type of law enforcement officer. Since going into business with Sal she has learned to spot the type straight away.

The man scans the room as if searching for danger; he doesn't even remove his sunglasses. He sees Camden at the front counter and takes a step in her direction, but halts immediately at the sight of the second man to enter the shop, a tall figure wearing a full-body Darth Vader costume. Even from across the room Camden can hear the eerie iron lung breathing sounds from the mask the man wears. The agent, and most of the customers, stare in disbelief.

Camden, however, is not shocked. She knows immediately that it's Sal, though what crazy scheme requires this costume she cannot begin to fathom. Sal has seen the agent as well, recognized him for what he is, and tenses visibly, though this only adds to the Vader effect. She has a brief vision of Sal in a holding cell explaining to the other inmates why he is dressed this way when the door chimes a third time.

An unknown cop and her cousin as Darth Vader standing in her bookstore on a bright, sunny day would normally be the most surreal thing Camden could envision. Her ex-husband, Giles Smoot, walking in at the very same time is simply more than her very logical, ordered mind can process. She leans forward and begins banging her head on the counter.

Everyone's attention turns to Camden now, and the efforts of Julia, who is also behind the counter, to stop her alarming behavior. Giles and the agent do not move, but Sal/Vader rushes forward.

"Cam," he shouts, his voice distorted and mechanical through the mask, "what the hell are you doing? Julia, take her upstairs."

Julia stares at him, only now realizing that it's Sal, and then pulls Camden to her feet. At that moment the agent steps forward.

"Hang on a minute," he says in a tone that indicates he is used to being obeyed without question. "I need to speak with Ms. Templeton."

Now every head turns to him. A few customers leave the store, clearly concerned about where this is heading. Julia freezes, and Camden looks up, but Sal moves toward the man rather than away from him. They would normally be the same height, but in his boots and Vader helmet Sal is six inches taller.

"Can you sons of bitches just leave me alone," he says, his voice menacing through the distortion.

This takes the agent by surprise, and he starts to speak, but Sal is just getting started.

"I mean seriously," he continues. "Does the goddam FBI have a department just working on pinning something on me? I'm a bookseller, for Christ's sake."

"And he was in Atlantic City that night," Julia adds helpfully. The agent tries unsuccessfully to hide a smile.

"Terranova," he says. "That's a different look for you. And I'm not FBI."

Sal pulls off the mask and stares hard at the man.

"Then who the hell are you?" he asks. "And why do you want to talk to my cousin?"

"Cosgrove," the man says, producing an identification card. "Special Agent Dalton Cosgrove."

Sal examines the card closely, and his eyes widen. He hands it back and glances at Camden and Julia, then back at Cosgrove.

"Homeland Security?" he asks. "What could Homeland Security possibly want with us?"

"Is there somewhere we can talk privately?" Cosgrove asks.

Sal nods, then motions for Camden to follow them to the office. However, she is staring past him at someone near the door.

"What about *him*?" she asks with more venom than Sal has ever heard from her.

"Who?" Sal asks, trying to see the man she is indicating.

"I think she means me," says a man with a clipped British accent. He steps forward and extends his hand. "Giles Smoot. I am Camden's ex-husband."

"Ah," Sal says, understanding her venom now. Then before he can stop himself he adds "At least you're wearing clothes this time."

Giles turns several shades of red, but nods in agreement. He is certainly not going to cause a scene with a government agent and a former gangster in Star Wars getup mere feet from him.

"Perhaps I should not have come unannounced," he says.

"Perhaps," Sal agrees, "But you're here now. Might as well hang around until we're done with Elliot Ness here. Julia, can you get Mr. Smoot a cup of coffee and show him to the Oscar Wilde section?"

Giles turns even redder, but simply mutters his thanks. Sal looks around the store at the remaining customers.

"Just a normal day here at The Last Word, folks," he says. "Everybody buy something. Fifty percent off all dead Russian authors for the next 30 minutes."

There is a howl of protest from Jacob Weinberg, who has only now stuck his head out the door of his rare book room. Sal laughs and ushers Camden and Cosgrove into the office.

The three of them are crammed into an office that barely fits two, what with the desk and bookcases and filing cabinets. Camden and Cosgrove sit in the only two chairs, while Sal perches on the edge of the desk. Camden is clearly still lost in thought over why Giles has suddenly appeared, but she snaps back to reality as soon as the agent begins speaking.

"Your store recently published a book," he says, looking down at a small notebook, "called *Bolivar, Guevara, and Beyond: A New Manifesto for Our Oppressed Latin Brothers*. Is that correct?"

"Obviously it's correct," Sal says, "or you wouldn't have it in your little book there. So what?"

"It has been brought to our attention that the book is not simply a work of history or politics, but is both subversive and inflammatory. At Homeland Security we take subversive and inflammatory seriously."

Camden looks from Cosgrove to Sal, obviously not grasping where this is going.

"I don't understand," she says to Cosgrove. "It's just a book. Why would you care about a book? Shouldn't you be —"

"Out beating Arab-Americans with clubs or water boarding Democrats or something?" Sal interjects.

Cosgrove is not amused, but he lets this pass.

"To be completely honest, we're not as concerned with the Sanchez boy, the co-author," he says, "as with the uncle, Ortiz. You may not be aware that you published a book by a man with an extensive criminal background and ties to the Puerto Rican independence movement."

"He is a decorated Army veteran!" Camden exclaims. "And the last time I looked, you Yanks had the freedom to belong to whatever political party you want, as well as freedom of the press."

"As for his 'extensive criminal background,'" Sal says, "to my knowledge the only time he was ever arrested was for a youthful indiscretion which led to him joining the

Army rather than doing jail time. Apparently he, like myself, is guilty until proven innocent with you guys."

Cosgrove puts aside any attempt at pleasantness now.

"I would expect someone like you to defend him, Terranova," he says. "But I am surprised by your reaction, Ms. Templeton. As the publisher of a book so blatantly at odds with the security of the United States –"

"Maybe you assholes should have been concerned about security *before* planes hit the Twin Towers," Sal says bitterly, rising to his feet. "I had friends who would be here today if you were as concerned with catching terrorists as you are with burning books."

Both Camden and Cosgrove are stunned by the vehemence of Sal's reaction. Cosgrove rises and Sal steps toward him, but Camden jumps between them.

"What exactly is it that you want, Agent Cosgrove?" she asks, keeping one eye on Sal.

"We want any information you can give us on Luis Ortiz' activities," he replies flatly.

"Oh, is that all?" Sal asks, suddenly calm, much too calm for Camden's liking. "I'll be glad to give you something that will help your investigation immensely."

Camden stares wide-eyed, and Cosgrove pulls out a pen and reopens his notebook.

"I'm ready," he says.

"Okay," Sal says. "Now write this down word for word. I don't want to be misquoted in your official report."

Cosgrove nods, his pen hovering over the paper.

"Go orally gratify a monkey. And get the hell out of my store."

Cosgrove glares at him for a long moment, then snaps the notebook shut and leaves without a word.

"Was that the best way to handle that?" Camden asks.

"Probably not," Sal admits, a smile spreading across his face, "but it sure felt good."

She looks him over as if she has finally noticed what he is wearing.

"Why in God's name are you dressed like that?" she asks.

"Halloween is right around the corner, cousin," he says as they walk back out to the sales floor. "And I have big plans for Halloween. But right now I have to talk to Ortiz, and you have to talk to Mr. Naked Badminton Player...sorry, I mean Mr. Smoot. Just keep him away from Ben."

"Very funny," she says.

"Hey, I'm not the one who couldn't tell my husband was gay. Hell, I could tell as soon as he walked in the door."

"Shut your face," she says. "And take off that stupid costume before you go out in public again."

"Hey, Julia," he shouts across the store. "Want to come upstairs and help me get out of my Darth Vader costume? We can play galactic conquest again."

"Nice try, Terranova," she yells back. "But you only got me into that Princess Leia metal bikini thing because I was drunk. Not happening again."

"Your loss," he replies, and then heads up the stairs.

3

"A Blast from the Past"

After Sal leaves to find Ortiz, Camden reluctantly leads Giles up to the apartment above the shop. She has not said a word to him, and is not certain she can without screaming. It had been his betrayal that led her here in the first place. Their marriage had ended more than a year ago when, the same morning she lost her job, she came home to find Giles and his much younger, male badminton partner naked at their kitchen table. She had left him, and London, and taken up the life of a bookseller in the States.

She motions for him to take a seat at the table, then says the only thing that comes to her mind.

"Cuppa?"

Giles nods but does not speak. She walks to the kitchen and puts on the kettle. A few minutes later she sets the cup of tea in front of him, takes her own, and sits down on the opposite side of the table.

"It's good," he says after taking a sip, giving her a weak, hesitant smile.

"Thank you," she replies. "Now what the bloody hell are you doing here?"

A few blocks away, Sal enters Billy McGee's, a glorified bar with excellent burgers. It is fortunate that Luis is here rather his normal haunt, The Blarney Stone, which owned by Jake Donovan's brother, Eddie. The drive to Arlington would have taken time, and Sal is not sure that time is a luxury they have.

Ortiz is seated at a booth in the back where he can see everyone who enters without immediately being seen himself. Sal knows this because he typically does the same thing, as well as always knowing where the exits are. But although Sal was urgent when they spoke on the phone, Ortiz appears completely relaxed; a Buddhist monk would not exude more calm. Sal slides into the booth across from him.

"Salvatore, my friend," Ortiz says as he motions to the waitress to bring two more beers, "what has you so troubled on this beautiful day? I hope there is nothing amiss with the lovely Camden."

"Actually, Cam does have some drama going on right now," Sal admits, "but I'm sure she can handle it. This is about you, Luis. A Homeland Security agent just came to the bookstore asking about you."

"Cosgrove has discovered my book," Ortiz says with a mischievous grin. "The powers that be do not appreciate great literature."

The waitress, who is very young and very attractive, returns and sets down the beers. Ortiz flashes a smile at her and she giggles, turns red, and hurries away.

"How do you do that?" Sal asks. "Any time a woman comes near you, you mesmerize them. It even works on Camden, which is saying something."

"With most it is simply my God-given Latin charisma," he replies in a matter-of-fact tone. "With the lovely Camden it is something much deeper, almost spiritual. But back to the inquisitive agent."

"Right," Sal says. "Apparently you know him."

"We have crossed paths a few times."

"Well I may not have helped you much with him. I was kind of belligerent."

"Kind of?" Ortiz asks, one eyebrow raised.

"When he asked us for information about you I basically called him a Fascist, and may have invited him to go blow a monkey before kicking him out of the store."

Ortiz roared with laughter, so loudly that several other diners looked over at them.

"Sal," he said admiringly, "you do have a problem with authority."

"True. But the authority isn't after me, not really. It's you they want."

"They have wanted me for a long time," Ortiz says, tenting his hands together in front of his lips as if in deep thought. "Yet they never seem to catch me."

"Why is that?" Sal asks. As one who has dodged the law most of his life, he is intrigued.

"Because, my friend, I do not want them to."

Giles takes a sip of tea before answering Camden's question, as if he's not quite sure how to say it. She is used to this; he has always been one to think through his words very carefully. Except that last time in the kitchen…her hands clench into fists involuntarily.

"I am in Dallas this week for a badminton tournament at the Park Cities Country Club," he says. "So I thought I would drop in and say hello."

"Is the Spencer boy still your partner?" she asks. She phrases it this way intentionally; he can't know if she means still his double partner in badminton or still his *partner*. The second possibility is why they are no longer married.

"He is here with me, yes," he says, finding a tactful way to answer both possibilities while answering neither.

"I see. You should have brought him round with you then. It would be a change to see him with his clothes on again."

"I had hoped we might be civil, Camden," he says.

"What in God's name would cause you to you hope that?" she asks, her voice rising. "And I ask again, Giles, why are you here? Dallas is not just round the corner from Fort Worth. You had to make an effort to be here."

Once again he does not answer immediately. *This must be something big*, she thinks.

"It seems that you will be staying here permanently," he says finally. "In America I mean."

"Yes," she says. "And that is not an answer."

"Quite. I was just thinking, if you weren't planning on coming back to England…it's just such a waste for them not to be used…I was hoping perhaps…"

At that moment it dawns on her, and her anger morphs into blind fury. She stands up so quickly that she knocks her chair over; it falls to the hardwood floor with a loud crack.

"You have balls, Giles Smoot," she says, "I'll give you that. But not in a million years would I give you and that…that…*boy*, my Arsenal season tickets."

"I never said give," he says, rising to his feet as well. "I would pay you for them, of course."

"My family has had those seats for decades," she replies. "No amount of money would be enough, and certainly not from you."

"Be reasonable," he says, his calm reserve slipping away. "You are five thousand miles away, your mum never goes to the matches anymore, and it will be ten years before my name gets to the top of the waiting list. Ten *years*."

"Don't worry," she says, "I'm sure Wenger will still be the manager then."

"Camden, honestly."

"Out," she says, pointing to the apartment door. "And if I ever see you again you will wish I hadn't."

He stares at her for a moment, then shrugs and leaves the apartment. She walks into her room and stares at the stadium seat Sal gave her as a Christmas present last year, stolen from Emirate's Stadium in North London before Arsenal had even begun playing matches there. She picks up her red and white Gunners scarf, which is draped across the seat and kisses it once. She had considered giving up the seats next season; now she will keep them forever, if only to delay Giles' name rising on the waiting list. For the first time since Cosgrove walked into the shop that day, Camden smiles.

4

"Football v. Futbol"

"It's time you learned about real football," Sal tells Camden as they are closing the shop one late September evening. "So we are going to watch a real live Texas High School Football Game tomorrow night."

"I know all about real football," she replies. "You people just call it soccer."

"Look, you come from a land of warm beer, funny TV shows, and small pasty guys who can kick a round ball. But if you're going to live here, which apparently you are, you have to make some concessions to the local customs. That includes chicken-fried steak, guns with Bible verses etched on the barrel, and high school football."

"I will go to a game after you've watched a soccer match," she counters.

"I watch them every Saturday," he says. "You have the Premier League on the TV first thing in the morning."

"You don't watch, you simply tolerate it being on."

"I got you the seat from the Emirate's for Christmas."

This was true. Sal had a friend steal her a seat from Arsenal's new home ground as a Christmas present. It was the best gift she had ever received.

"And," he continues, "in case you have forgotten, I did watch most of a match with you our first summer here."

"What match?"

"Italy against France," he says. "The World Cup final."

Damn it. How could she have forgotten that? Camden thinks back to the day, and all in all it was a fairly comical experience.

"What do you mean you're showing a baseball game?" Camden had screamed into the phone that day. "It's the bloody World Cup final!" She slammed the phone down and looked over at Sal, who shrugged.

"I told you," he said. "No one cares about the World Cup here, especially since the US isn't in the final."

"But seriously," she said, "a baseball game between the Dodgers and the Nets?"

"I think you mean *Mets*," Sal corrected. "See, you know even less about baseball than I do about soccer."

"I know there won't be almost a billion people worldwide watching baseball today," she retorted. On this point he could not disagree.

"Why do you care anyway?" he asked, taking a different approach in hopes of ending this conversation. "England was eliminated a week ago. I know this not because I care about your silly game where no one dives on a loose ball – un-American, by the way – but because you got drunk and sobbed late into the night."

"To the Portuguese," she said bitterly. "And on penalties. Again."

"Whatever that means," Sal said. "My point is, you're English, England is out, move on with life. Trust me; I'm a Jets fan, so I understand losing. Maybe go sell a book or two so we don't lose the store."

"It's the final of the bloody *World Cup*," Camden replied in a tone that threatened to rise into a scream again. "I have to watch it."

"Fine," he said. "So none of the sports bars you called are showing it?"

"Not one. Baseball, golf, and something called NASCAR, which I can only assume is an American version of Formula One."

Sal tried not to laugh at this last part; it would only anger her more. Then he had a thought. "Who is playing in the final?" he asked.

"Italy and France." Her expression when she said *France* was that of someone forced to swallow a mixture of broken glass and cat urine. Not a fan, obviously.

"Then my advice is that you call around to the Italian restaurants," he said. "Even though most of the ones here are actually run by Lebanese and Albanians, I bet they will show the game in the bar area to at least appear authentically Italian. And I suppose Lebanese and Albanians like soccer more than baseball."

She stared at him wide-eyed, and then a smile spread across her face. "That is brilliant!" she said happily, snatching up the phone again. "A simply brilliant idea, Sal."

He walked to the kitchen for a beer while she dialed. Sal had thought that running the bookstore he and Camden had recently inherited would be the difficult part, but sharing the apartment above the store with his English cousin had proven even trickier. He walked back into the living room to find her beaming.

"Napoli's is showing it!" she exclaimed. "And the man on the phone said their bar has a big screen TV."

"See," Sal said, "it all worked out just fine."

"Do you want to come watch it with me?" she asked.

He knew he should say "yes," but he couldn't. Anything – baseball, golf, NASCAR, watching paint dry – would be preferable to watching a bunch of Italians and Frenchmen kick a ball around for two hours, score one time, and then call the game "a classic."

"I would," he said, "but I need to rearrange the fiction section downstairs." This was not untrue; it had needed rearranging for weeks. "You could ask Julia."

"No, she asked for the afternoon off," Camden said. "It's her mother's birthday or something. And Heather has to cover for her, so she's out too."

"What about –" Sal began, but Camden cut him off.

"Do not suggest that I take Jacob with me," she said.

"I was going to suggest Kate," he replied. "She always closes her shop early on Sundays anyway."

Camden pondered this for a moment, seemed to find it acceptable, and picked up the phone again. Sal finished the beer and quickly left the apartment, just in case.

As they entered Napoli's a few hours later, it was clear who the soccer fan was. While Kate was dressed in a t-shirt, shorts and sandals, Camden looked like a walking billboard for the England National Team. She wore a David Beckham jersey, which was forgivable both because he was the England captain and because he had left the hated Manchester United for Real Madrid. Real Madrid was also hated, but they didn't play Arsenal twice a season. Her England kit shorts bore the number 3; this was Ashley Cole's number, and he *was* an Arsenal player. In spite of the heat, she wore an England scarf, and had painted the St. George's Cross on her face. Kate had not known this was the flag of England, having only ever seen the Union Jack before.

"You take this soccer thing seriously," Kate said once they were seated at a small table in front of the television.

"No more than fans of American sports do here," Camden replied with naïve sincerity.

"Camden, honey," she said sweetly, patting Camden's hand, "here only the college kids paint their faces. And only when their team is playing."

"Really? How odd."

A waitress took their order, trying unsuccessfully to keep a straight face when looking at Camden. Kate glanced around the bar; there were only a few other patrons, none of whom had team jerseys or painted faces.

"So is it common in England?" Kate asked.

"Oh yes," Camden replied. "We're not as passionate about the national squad as our club teams, but only because we've had our hearts broken so many times since '66." She said this as if she had even been alive the one and only time England had won the Cup.

"Club teams?" Kate asked, confused.

"In the Premier League," Camden said. "It's like your NFL, I suppose. The loyalty to a club gets passed down generation to generation. I got it from my mum, since dad was a Yank and only came to the game later in life."

"Your *mother* raised you to go out in public like this?" Kate asked, shocked.

"Oh no," Camden said. "Mum would be scandalized if she knew I wear a Beckham jersey. Only Arsenal players for her. When I was a little girl she ran an antique shop and absolutely refused to sell to anyone who was a Tottenham supporter."

"I assume that is a rival," Kate said. "But how would she know?"

"She asked them right out of the gate. No Manchester United fans either. For the Liverpool and Chelsea fans she just charged a higher price."

The waitress returned with their drinks, stared at Camden for a moment, and left.

"So who is playing again?" Kate asked.

"Italy and France," Camden said. "Or as we would say back home, Italy and the Cheese Eating Surrender Monkeys."

"Who won last year?" Kate asked. Camden wasn't sure she had heard her right.

"Say again?"

"Who won the World Cup last year?"

"It's only played every four years, Kate."

"Oh, like the Olympics." Kate shifted uneasily in her chair. "I have to confess something," she said, her eyes not meeting Camden's.

"What?" Camden asked, suddenly a bit worried.

"The thing is, I don't know anything at all about what we're about to watch."

"That's no problem," she said with a smile. "I can explain it all before the match even starts. The World Cup is played every four years. Nearly 200 national teams compete to be in the finals, which is pared down to 32 teams for the final tournament, which takes a month. They start with eight groups of four teams each who play the teams within their group; the top two from each group move on to the knockout stage, and from there it's a simple tournament format. England was eliminated in the quarterfinals."

Kate nodded as if this all made perfect sense, and then their attention was drawn to the television screen. The teams were walking out of the tunnel and onto the field. In the Berlin stadium nearly 70,000 fans roared, all dressed as colorfully as Camden.

Seven minutes into the match, France took the lead on a penalty kick by the humorously named (in Kate's opinion) Zinedine Zidane. "Bloody frogs," was all Camden said. Before play resumed, Kate had another confession.

"Camden," she said sheepishly, "when I said that I didn't know anything about what we were about to watch, I didn't mean the World Cup, at least not exactly that."

"What then?" Camden asked, trying to look at Kate and the screen at the same time.

"I meant I know nothing about soccer."

Camden's head whipped around. "Nothing?"

"Well, I know that you're supposed to kick the ball in the net, and that you're not allowed to touch it with your hands. Except for the tall guy standing in front of the net – why is his jersey a different color? – and when it goes out of bounds, but it doesn't look like that's always true either."

Camden was about to reply when the bartender reached up and changed the channel. Suddenly they were watching baseball. Camden shot out of her chair like a missile.

"What do you think you're doing?" she snarled.

"The Mets are playing the Dodgers," he said, still facing the screen. Then he turned, saw the murderous look on her painted face, and changed it back without a word. She returned to the table.

Just as their third round of drinks arrived, Italy pulled even on a header by Marco Materazzi off a corner kick. Camden tried to explain the concept of set pieces to Kate, but she giggled like a teenager every time Camden said the word "header." Perhaps the third drink was too much for her.

The match remained deadlocked through the end of regular time, and Camden could see that Kate was getting bored as the most exciting part was approaching: extra time. It was possible that they might even remain tied after that and have to decide the champion on penalty kicks. As an England supporter, the mere thought of a penalty shootout made her want to punch a French nun and then throw up.

During extra time Kate started whining.

"Is this going to be over soon?" she asked, slurring her words. "I have to open the bakery at 5 in the morning."

"Yes," Camden replied, irritated that she nearly missed an amazing save by the Italian keeper Buffon, who just tipped a Zidane shot over the crossbar.

Just as Kate was about to start yammering again, Camden was saved by the most unlikely person: Sal. He appeared from nowhere, beer in hand, and pulled a chair up to the table. Kate's protests ceased immediately, replaced by a dreamy look as she stared at him.

"What are you doing here?" Camden asked. "I thought games where you don't dive on a loose ball were un-American."

"They are," Sal replied. "But after I closed up the bookstore I started feeling guilty, as an Italian. I should at least make a token effort to cheer for the homeland."

She turned to look at him, and saw his eyes grow wide. She spun back to the television.

"What?" she asked, fearing that the Frogs had scored. An Italian player was on the ground, Zidane standing over him.

"The bald guy just head-butted one of my *paisanos*," he said, amazed.

Sure enough, the referee was racing toward Zidane, a red card held high over his head. Zidane looked defiant, then defeated.

"What does that little card mean?" Kate asked.

"He's been sent off!" Camden nearly squealed with glee.

"Sent off?" Kate said. The alcohol had definitely impaired her.

"The Frenchy got tossed out," Sal translated. "Deserved it too. So does that mean we win?"

"No," Camden said, exasperated. "It means they have to play with only ten men now."

"That's a shame," Sal said, motioning to the waitress for another beer. "I was hoping it was over."

It was not over. After neither side scored in extra time, it did indeed come down to a penalty shootout. It was almost anticlimactic after the Zidane head-butt, but the Italians won the shootout 5-3. Everyone at the table had been pleased: Sal that the Italians had won, Camden that the French had lost, and Kate that it was over and she could go to bed.

"I can tell by the faraway look in your eye," Sal says, "that you are fantasizing about David Beckham, which means you remember, since you were wearing his jersey. So tomorrow night at 7:00 you will get your first experience with the thing people here care more about than pretty much anything."

"Who else is going?" she asks. "And what teams are we watching?"

"Julia will be there, and I asked Ortiz to come if he's free so you wouldn't feel like a third wheel. Heather, Ben and Jacob will mind the store with a couple of the Sirens."

"They have names, you know," Camden says.

"I know. As for the teams, I have chosen the best possible contest, one that ups the ante on the already abnormally high stakes. We will be watching Pope Pius XII High School do battle with Briarwood Christian Academy; Catholics vs. Baptists, just like God intended."

The parking lot is already full the following night, and Sal searches for several minutes for a parking spot as far away from other cars as possible. He has only recently purchased a cherry, midnight black 1967 Mustang, and is paranoid about someone bumping, dinging, scratching, or even breathing on it. As they approach the stadium, aptly named Our Lady of Victory, Camden marvels at its size. It looks as large as a Premier League stadium back home.

"How big is their stadium?" she asks.

"It can hold 40,000 spectators," Luis says. "I know this because my niece Imelda attends school here, and she was outraged that they would spend such an amount on a football stadium when there are homeless people in Fort Worth. She called it un-Catholic. All of my family is very socially conscious, as you know."

Camden begins laughing uncontrollably, which Luis misinterprets as her mocking his family's commitment to social causes. She sees his expression change and regains control of herself and puts a hand on his arm.

"I'm not laughing at what you said, Luis," she assures him. "It's just funny to me that a high school stadium is bigger than White Hart Lane."

"You're comparing a stadium to a street?" Julia asks, confused.

"No," Cam says. "White Hart Lane is the name of the stadium where Tottenham Hotspur play; it only holds around 36,000."

Julia gives her a quizzical look. "Don't ask," Sal tells her.

"I assume that's another of your soccer teams, but why is it so funny?" she asks anyway. Sal shakes his head and quickens his pace, pulling away from them.

"Tottenham are definitely not one of my teams," Camden answers testily, "and it's funny because they are Arsenal's most hated rival. By comparison, the new Emirates Stadium holds over 70,000."

"That's the one we gave you the seat from, right?" Julia asks.

"Yes," Camden replies, her smile returning.

They find seats on the home side of the stadium, choosing their allegiance based solely on Ortiz's niece; Sal is Catholic and Julia a Baptist, so they cancel out each other's vote. The crowd is boisterous, as you would expect from thousand of teenagers and their equally overzealous parents. Camden is pleased to see that a few of the kids have even painted their faces in their respective school colors.

"Now remember, Cam," Sal says into her ear. "Everyone is allowed to touch the ball in this game. The only ones who use their feet are called, appropriately, the kicker and the punter."

"Back home we call gamblers punters, and also members of an audience," she replies.

"Two great cultures," Sal says, "divided by a common language and a big ocean."

"Like Spain and Latin America and Puerto Rico," Ortiz says. The fact that he does not include Puerto Rico in Latin America is not lost on Sal.

"I thought Spanish was the same everywhere," Julia says.

"Oh no, my dear Julia," Ortiz says. "The pure form is spoken only in the Spanish region of Castile and on my home island of Puerto Rico."

"Of course," she says with a smile.

"Where are the songs?" Camden asks, completely changing the subject to something clearly more important to her.

"Songs?" Sal asks. "What do you mean, the school fight song?"

"No, the songs, the chants," she says. "In England every team's supporters have songs that encourage our lads and insult our opponents. Do they not have that here?"

"We have insults," Julia says, "but they are usually fairly tame at the high school games."

"Boring," Camden says.

During halftime, while the marching bands are playing, Sal does his best to explain to Camden what has been going on. He tried explaining during the game, but that proved too difficult.

"It's my own fault," he says loudly, trying to be heard over the horns and drums. "I should have given you an American Football 101 class before we left the store."

"It just seems so complicated," she says. "Besides the fact that they wear more armor than knights in a jousting tournament, they run for one minute and then rest for another minute trying to move ten yards down the field. Unlike real football, where you run non-stop for 45 minutes a half. Those poor, huge boys in the front just wrestle with each other every play, while the skinny boys run past everyone with the ball. And why in the world are there so many ways to score, and why do you get six points for some things, three for others, and one for that extra kick nonsense?"

Sal shakes his head at the sheer number of things she does not understand, though trying to see it from her perspective he has to admit it can get confusing.

"Listen up, Limey," he says. "You get six points for a touchdown; that's when you cross your opponent's goal line with the ball. You get three for a field goal, where the kicker kicks it through the goalpost. The extra point, what you called an extra kick, only comes after a touchdown."

"I understand the lovely Camden's confusion," Ortiz says. "My Latin heritage makes me love futbol, yet there is something noble and glorious in the gladiatorial combat that is American football."

"Real football just makes so much more sense," she argues. "One point for one goal. Simple. And there's something else I don't get. If this is a game between two schools, why are all of the kids hanging out by the concession stand and in the parking lot, yet their parents are screaming like this is a life or death struggle?"

"Parents here have an unfortunate tendency to attempt to relive their youth through their children," Julia says.

"But with such vehemence?" Camden asks. "I thought that poor referee was going to be assaulted a minute ago."

"Says the woman who comes from the country that invented soccer hooligans," Sal says.

The teams return to the field before she can respond, and the second half begins. Camden tries, really tries, to follow the action and understand not only what is going on, but why so many Americans love this game as much as she loves soccer, why it dominates the culture from September to January, why Sal forces poor Julia to watch those horrible New York Jets play. But despite her best effort, she just doesn't get it, and as the final whistle blows, she thinks she understands why.

Tonight's game was a close one; St. Pius won by a score of 31 – 28. But in reality, St. Pius only executed five scoring plays (not counting those silly extra kicks): four touchdowns and one field goal. Briarwood managed four scoring plays: four touchdowns. In a sensible scoring system, the final score would have been 5 – 4, or something like that. Yet just like all the protective gear they wear to make the game look more dramatic, the score was inflated to make it seem bigger than it really was. America, she decides, is simply a place that likes being big and doing big things.

She does not say any of this to Sal, who can become shockingly patriotic at the oddest moments. Rather she files this little nugget of insight away for later use; she is sure she will need it at some point during her bookselling sojourn in Her Majesty's Former Colonies.

5

"Another Surprise Guest"

Camden is not a morning person. In spite of this, she wakes at 5:00 a.m. every day, weekends and holidays included, and has done so since she was 15 years old; it's a self-discipline thing. One of the effects of this early rising is that though, as a proper English woman she prefers tea, mornings are started with coffee, the stronger the better.

This morning she can smell the coffee already brewing in the kitchen, which means that Sal must already be awake. The timer on the coffee pot broke a few weeks ago, and she hasn't gotten around to buying a new one yet. This strikes her as odd, though, because Sal is never up this early, unless he's just getting in from the night before.

Camden throws a thick bathrobe over the XL-sized Arsenal T-shirt she uses as a nightshirt, walks out to the kitchen, and screams. A man who is most definitely not Sal is standing there, and her scream causes him to jump; he drops his coffee mug in the process. The sound it makes as it crashes to the hardwood floor is as loud as her scream.

At that moment Sal appears from his bedroom wearing only a pair of old gym shorts bearing the logo of the New York Jets. He is holding a Glock 9mm pistol.

"What the hell?" he yells, clearly still groggy.

Camden backs toward her bedroom door and simply points at the stranger in the kitchen. He has not moved, likely frozen in place by the menacing sight of her cousin and his large gun. The man slowly raises his hands and gives Sal a questioning look. Not frightened, she realizes, but questioning. As if they know each other.

"Who is this man?" she demands, pointing at the stranger, but looking at Sal. "And why is he in my kitchen at five in the morning?"

Sal lowers the gun, and the main hesitantly lowers his hands.

"*Our* kitchen," he replies, then walks to the cupboard and pulls down three mugs. "He's a friend of mine. Actually, I'm more of a fan than a friend. He's going to crash here for a few days while he gets some things sorted out."

Her expression would show less amazement if he told her he was training monkeys to ride unicycles while juggling chainsaws.

"Pardon?" she says.

"Let's all sit down and I will explain everything," he assures her, but she is not reassured. The stranger likewise appears skeptical, but Sal pours coffee for each of them and ushers them into the stylish but uncomfortable wooden chairs around the kitchen table.

The man is still staring at the Glock, which Sal has set beside him on the table. Sal notices this and quickly moves it. The man relaxes slightly.

"Start explaining, Terranova," Camden says after taking a sip of coffee, her eyes now on the stranger. "And this better be good."

"Right," he says, then takes a drink from his own mug. "Camden, this is Max Luther. Max, this is my cousin and business partner, Camden Templeton."

They nod at each other and Max extends his hand. Camden reluctantly shakes it.

"Max is a writer of some note," Sal continues. Max visibly reddens at this declaration. Camden's attitude toward him softens immediately. "He has written several novels that, while not always commercial hits, are simply brilliant. You wouldn't know him, of course, partial as you are to non-fiction and trashy romance novels."

She reaches over to slap the back of his head, but this being a common occurrence he deftly dodges the blow.

"Anyway," Sal continues, "By a stroke of luck I met Max last night at a gallery showing on 7th Street."

"Wait," she interrupts. "Why were you at a gallery showing?"

"I like art," he replies defensively. "I am far more cultured than you realize."

"Julia made you go with her," Camden says with a slight grin.

"I accompanied her at her request, yes. Focus…we're not talking about me."

"Continue."

"So I met Mr. Luther last night at the gallery, where it happened he had ducked in to escape the thunderstorms that rolled through."

"I smelled tacos," Max says; it is the first time he's spoken. His voice is deeper than Camden had expected.

"Yeah," Sal says with a nod. "The Tex-Mex buffet was easily the best thing there. I don't like abstract paintings. A sailboat should, I don't know, look like a freaking sailboat."

"Focus," Camden says.

"Well, we started talking because I recognized him from the jacket photo of his first novel, *Liquid Time*, and in the course of the conversation learned that he needed a place to stay temporarily."

"I'm between things right now," Max says, looking down into his cup.

"Between things?" Camden repeats.

"Between books, between publishers, agents, wives, dwellings," he clarifies, still not looking up.

"Max was living in Brooklyn," Sal explains, "but rents there are astronomical, and it's cold in the winter, and he heard that the literary scene here was jumping."

"Literary scene? In Fort Worth?" Camden almost spits out her coffee, she is laughing so hard. "There is no literary scene here."

"I was misinformed," Max says, finally looking up and smiling at Camden. He has a great smile.

"Perhaps," Sal says. "But we're going to change that, starting today."

Camden stares blankly at him; Sal's schemes are always interesting, often catastrophic, occasionally illegal, and on rare occasions blasphemous. His recent attempt to turn the store into a "church" was at least three of the four. Sal, however, simply smiles.

She looks at Max, taking him in completely for the first time. He is in his 50s and has not shaved for several days. The stubble on his cheeks is more white than black, which surprises her given that he is only slightly gray at the temples. His hair hangs past his collar, wavy and in need of a cut. His most striking feature, aside from a small scar under his left eye, is the eyes themselves. They have seemed to change color several times, from hazel when she first saw him to almost gray to a deep brown when he looked up from his coffee. He is tall, over six feet, but too thin. Camden thinks he has been "between things" for more than a few days.

"I appreciate you letting me stay here last night," Max says, in general rather than to either of them specifically. "And I apologize for scaring you ma'am. I can see you're not comfortable with me staying here, so I'll be on my way."

His eyes are definitely deep brown now, and turning him away would be like abandoning a lost puppy. She glances at Sal, who gives a quick nod.

"You just startled me," she says. "It's no trouble if you need to stay for a few days." *Unless you turn out to be an ax murderer or an escapee from a lunatic asylum.* She suddenly has a thought, something that can confirm this stranger is who Sal thinks he is. "Would we have any of your books in the store?"

Max shrugs and gestures to Sal.

"I ordered some before I went to bed last night," he says. "None in the store proper, but I have all of them on my shelves up here. And now they're signed." He beams like a kid with a new bike.

It amazes her than someone as hard as Sal, who has lived outside the law most of his life, can be so star-struck. Springsteen, Lucky Luciano, and now Max Luther; quite the assortment of heroes. She finishes her coffee and stands; Max stands as well, Sal does not.

"Apparently chivalry and gentlemanly manners are alive and well," she says, "everywhere except Jersey. It's been a pleasure meeting you, Mr. Luther."

"Max," he replies. "Just Max. And the pleasure was all mine, I assure you."

She blushes slightly at this; she has never been good at receiving compliments. "I need to get ready for work," she says. "Sal, you can fill me in on this grand plan of yours at lunch."

"Grand doesn't begin to cover it," he says. "This town will never be the same."

That's exactly what she is afraid of.

"It's your basic two-pronged strategy," Sal says later that day as they eat sandwiches at a small table in the break room at the back of the store.

"I still can't believe you let a stranger stay in your apartment," Julia says, completely ignoring his statement.

"He's not a stranger," Sal says. "He is a well-known author."

"Not that well-known," she replies. "He could be a serial killer, or a thief, or something."

"I think I can spot a thief," he says with a smile. She can't argue with that. "And I'm a good judge of character." That is more questionable.

"And where is he now?" she asks. "On your couch watching game shows?"

"I thought I was the cynic here," he says. "No, he is actually at Benny's Beans drinking coffee, reading

Hemingway, and working on his new novel. Later today we'll go by the Greyhound station and get his bags from the locker and come back here. You can meet him then."

"Did I hear someone say Hemingway?" Heather asks as she enters the room.

"Easy there," Sal says. "No one is reading Papa out loud or anything, so don't get excited." She flips him off and leaves the room. "Such respect from my employees," he says.

"Anyway," Camden says, trying to steer the conversation back on course, "you were talking about a two-pronged strategy of some sort."

"Yes, two-pronged," Sal says, clearly enjoying the phrase. "The first is the most obviously lacking around here: a book festival. Fort Worth needs a book festival."

"Say again?" Camden asks, but Julia is already nodding in agreement.

"A book festival," Sal repeats. "Good lord, woman, you should know about these things. After all, the London Book Fair is one of the biggest in the world."

"After Frankfurt," Julia adds helpfully.

"I was an accountant," Camden replies, drawing out each syllable of the word accountant. "I thought book fairs would be boring."

"Wrong yet again," he says. "Ours would be different than London or Frankfurt, of course. Nearly all publishers and booksellers are at the big fairs. We don't necessarily need that. We just need the authors and their books. Publishers would be gravy."

"And people to read them," Julia says. "So more like the Sundance Arts Festival or North Texas Film Festival."

"Exactly," Sal agrees. "Though I didn't know we had an arts festival."

"Yeah, you're a big art fan," Camden says. "The problem is that those have been going on for years, decades even, and have a fan base already. We would have to start out much smaller even than those."

"Perhaps," Sal says. "The important thing is to start."

"I'm on it," Julia says without hesitation.

Sal nods. He had hoped she would say this, being far more organized than he is and more creative than Camden.

"However," she continues, ""something like this is best held in the spring, and it requires proper planning; not thrown together like your little Hemingway fiasco."

"It was not a fiasco," he says defensively. "It was energetic. It will be even better the next time."

"Whatever," Julia says, not even attempting to humor him on this one. "In any case, it will take time to put together the right way."

"Fine," he says, though he is clearly not fine with it. Sal likes things to happen quickly.

"And prong number two?" Camden asks, relieved that his first idea was neither insane nor illegal. Sal hesitates a moment before answering, which is never a positive sign.

"Shakespeare and Company," he says. She waits for him to elaborate, but apparently this is the entire answer.

"What does that even mean?" She asks. "You've told me about Sylvia Beach, and I know her picture hangs above the counter – patron saint of booksellers and all that – but what does she have to do with us in the present day?"

Before Sal can answer, Julia jumps in.

"I think I get it," she says excitedly. "Sylvia wasn't just a bookseller; she was a patron of the literary scene in Paris. She took care of the writers like they were her children, loaned them books, loaned them money, let them have their mail delivered to the store, read their manuscripts, and finally began publishing them when no one else would. Is that the kind of thing you're talking about?"

Sal nods happily. Julia gets it, gets him. But there is more.

"Yes," he says, "but that's only one part of what Shakespeare and Company means."

"So there are three prongs," Camden says, particularly concerned about the 'loaned writers money' part of what Julia has just said.

"Call it 2a and 2b," Sal says. "Sylvia closed the shop during the German occupation and never reopened. But in the 1950s a man named George Whitman – no relation to either Walt or that woman who wrote *The Forbidden Fruit* – opened an English language bookstore in Paris and named it Shakespeare and Company as well. It's still open today, run by his daughter, Sylvia Beach Whitman."

"He named his daughter after Sylvia Beach?" Camden asks.

"Yes he did. And to think you'd never even heard of her until a year ago."

"Wait a minute, Sal," Julia says. "I know about George Whitman. I read a memoir about his store a couple years ago. You aren't suggesting –"

"I am suggesting," he says firmly.

"That would be chaos," Julia replies. "It would never work, not in America, and definitely not in Fort Worth."

"What are you two on about?" Camden asks.

"He wants to let authors live in the store," Julia says. "Whitman saw his store as a socialist Utopia or something."

"*Live* in the store?" Camden asks, staring at Sal in disbelief.

"Live here and work on their books too," he says. "Why not?"

"You're mad as pants," she replies. Camden still reverts to British expressions when she is especially flustered.

"Shakespeare and Company, Bloomsbury…we could be that today," Sal insists. He then produces the very book Julia had been talking about, a memoir by Jeremy Mercer about his year living at Shakespeare and Company, and hands it to Camden.

"Just read it and think about it," he says. "You'll probably like it. It's non-fiction."

There is an uncomfortable silence until Julia pushes away from the table and stands.

"Well," she says as lightly as she can, "back to work."

"Yeah," Sal says, still staring at Camden. "I should probably go check on Max. He is a stranger in a strange land down here. I know what that's like."

Camden says nothing. She simply opens the book and starts reading the first page, completely ignoring Sal. She is still reading long after both of them have gone.

6

"The Writer in His Natural Habitat"

Coffee shops are the same the world over, Max thinks as he gazes around the interior of Benny's Beans. Whether in Brooklyn or Berlin, Fresno or Fort Worth, the smell of the coffee permeates, students act like they're studying, and small cliques discuss their world, from politics to music to the cost of babysitters. The familiarity calms him.

Max has never been able to write in complete silence; he avoids libraries except for the most essential research. Nor can he work if there is too much noise, so bars and restaurants don't work either, not that they are places a normal person would write in any case. But coffee houses, even the big chain versions that had pushed so many mom and pop establishments out of business over the years, are perfect. The background music is typically jazz or folk (in keeping with the hipster appearance), played softly. The conversations are muted enough that when mingled with each other they result in a white noise that is exactly what Max needs in order to work.

He needs it more now than ever, because the block that started several months ago in Brooklyn has travelled south with him. Although to be honest, the results had not been that impressive when he had been writing, at least not for a long time. Max thinks back to the conversation from this morning. Sal had mentioned *Liquid Time* and the jacket photo from that debut novel. Both the book and the picture are three decades old now, and how anyone could recognize him from either is a mystery.

He takes a sip of his coffee, black with cream, and flips open his Moleskin journal. He had started using them because Hemingway had, hoping that the Great American Novel was only as far away as the right notebook. It hadn't worked out that way, of course, but he had filled hundreds of them over the years nonetheless.

The novel he is working on now has little chance of convincing a new agent or publisher to take him on; no vampires or zombies, very little romance, no way to turn it into a blockbuster movie franchise. Woody Allen might have liked it, but Woody wrote all his own stuff. Still, Max has stuck to writing what he wants to write, rather than chasing the hot trend, his whole life, and there is no way he's changing that now.

He peers out of the corner of his eye, watching a pair of young mothers who have been discussing the best Christian preschools for their toddlers. Is there something there he can use? Surely not a complete character, but perhaps a trait, a snippet of conversation, a gesture he has never noticed before.

People often ask Max, or had when he was still relevant enough to be asked, where he got his characters. Not his ideas…his characters, the implication being that writers simply take some real person's life and transcribe it onto the page. This was almost never the case, unless you wanted to end up in court.

His reply is always the same: everywhere. And it's the truth; everyone you meet, see, hear about, read about, whatever, can sneak into the personality of your characters. Even when you don't want them to. Thus, his newest protagonist is a burned-out novelist convinced that he was born too late, trapped in a world where words hardly matter and the correct use of words matters not at all.

He looks up from his coffee to see that a young woman has taken a seat across from him at his table. She is staring at him as if she has seen a ghost.

"Can I help you?" he asks.

"You look a lot like Max Luther," she replies, her voice shaky. She is probably still in college, and perhaps she was forced to read *Liquid Time* or even *Midnight in Trafalgar Square* by a sadistic literature professor and wants to berate him for it.

"That's because I am," he says.

"You can't be," he says, shaking her head violently. This is not the response he expects. An autograph request maybe, or a question about the motivation of a character, but certainly not this.

"Excuse me?" he says.

"You cannot be Max Luther," she says again. "You look like him, sure, but you just can't be."

"And why not?"

"Because if you are, I just failed my Contemporary Lit class."

"I don't understand," he says. Maybe the young lady is already drunk at this early hour.

"I did a paper on your novel *Liquid Time*," she explains, still staring at him in disbelief. "I didn't like it much, by the way. The assignment required that I include a mini bio of the author, and according to Wikipedia you died of a heart attack two months ago."

"Really?" he asks, truly surprised. He shouldn't be though; Wikipedia was the single most unreliable source of knowledge this side of *The National Enquirer*. "I think I would remember if I had died, don't you?"

"Whatever," she says. "The point is, it will look really bad saying you're dead if you're not."

"Sorry," he says. It's all he can think of.

"Yeah, well sorry won't keep me from having to repeat the class. And I am not sleeping with that professor again. I did that for the midterm and only got a C."

"Well, it is possible I could die before your teacher grades it," he says helpfully.

"A nice thought," she says, "but I'm not that lucky." With that she stands and walks out the door. He decides that this scene will make it into the book word-for-word. *Dead?* That would certainly explain a few things.

He returns to his notebook; he has written nothing since coming in here. He has listened…no, eavesdropped is a better word…to conversations, watched people, read a few chapters of *A Farewell to Arms* for the hundredth time, but no real work has taken place.

Another person has stopped at his table. He looks up, hoping it's not another co-ed angry that he is alive. It is Sal, holding a cup of coffee and a plate with three chocolate croissants. He sets the plate in front of Max, who eats one immediately, thanking him after he takes the last bite.

"So what are you working on now?" Sal asks as he takes a seat across from Max. "Or should I not ask?"

"You can ask," Max says, "but there's not much to tell." Max looks at the remaining croissant; Sal has one in his hand already. Sal pushes the plate closer to Max, who smiles and thanks him again.

"Writer's block?" Sal asks.

"Something like that," Max answers through a mouthful of croissant. "I just can't find a main character, one that *moves* me."

"I don't know enough about how that whole creative process stuff works to offer much encouragement," Sal says. "I read, but I sure as hell can't write." He lights a cigarette and inhales deeply.

"You can't smoke in here," Max says, alarmed that Sal is doing just that.

"I know," he replies, taking another drag.

A large man behind the counter, presumably the "Benny" of Benny's Beans, yells across the room at Sal.

"Hey Terranova, you can't smoke in here."

"I know, Benny," Sal yells back. "And in another couple drags I won't be. Be a sport and bring me an ashtray."

Max stares hard at Sal for a long moment, as if seeing him clearly for the first time since they met.

"Who *are* you?" he asks Sal.

"I'm Sal," he replies. "We met last night, remember? You crashed at my apartment, freaked out my cousin, etc."

"I know that," Max says in an exasperated tone. "And you're a fan, blah blah blah. But who are you really, because you are not the typical bookseller."

"No, you're right about that. I came to this noble profession quite late after a career of questionable legitimacy back East."

Max's eyes widen and his mouth drops open; he finally recognizes him.

"You're Sally Fingers," he says, more loudly than he intended. No one in the coffee shop seems to notice, but he immediately regrets saying it.

"Some called me that at one time," Sal says, still smiling.

"And the thing in Ithaca?" Max asks.

"I was in Albany at the time," Sal says. "No, it was Altoona. Damn, where is Julia when I need her? It started with an A…"

"Atlantic City?" Max suggests.

"Yes!" Sal exclaims. "Atlantic City. I really need to remember that better."

"But now you sell books?" Max asks. "That's quite a career change."

"It was precipitated by a misunderstanding with someone's mother and facilitated by the untimely demise of a favorite uncle. But I like it."

"You like it better here than the City?" Max asks, incredulous, but not missing the fact that Sal certainly doesn't talk like your average thug. As a New Yorker, Max refers to New York City simply as the City.

"Nothing beats New York," Sal says, his smile fading a bit. "But then I wasn't in the City when I left. I was in Trenton."

"Oh," Max says with a knowing nod.

"Yeah, Fort Worth is definitely better than Trenton. But look, we can exchange life histories later. I need to let you work." He starts to get up, but an idea flashes in Max's mind, and he stops him.

"I wonder," Max says, his brain suddenly working at a fever pitch.

"Wonder what?" Sal asks.

"It might not work, and you might not even agree."

"You'd be surprised what I'll agree to," Sal says. "Tell me."

"What if I wrote about you?"

Sal is silent.

"What?" Max asks, suddenly worried again. "Did I say something wrong?"

"I don't think I can agree to that," Sal says, a bit sadly Max thinks. "There are certain statutes that have, shall we say, not yet reached their limitations, if you get my meaning."

Max laughs so hard he almost chokes on his coffee. He could use Sal's dialogue verbatim, and probably would if he wasn't afraid of waking up with a horse's head on his pillow.

"I'm not talking about a biography, Sal," he explains. "I'm a novelist. But your story, and you as the basis for a character, could work."

"Burglar to bookseller," Sal says, something he has said in his mind many times.

"Yes, maybe. Something along those lines at least."

"I'll have to think on that some," Sal says, and this time he does get up. "If you're looking for characters, we've got plenty of those. Come back with me and I'll introduce you to some. Besides, I have a proposition for you as well."

"I think he's lost his mind," Camden says to Julia and Andrea (whom Sal persists in calling Siren One as their uncle had). She would say the same to Sal himself, if he ever comes back from retrieving his writer. He has been gone for hours.

"I think he's just bored," Julia says. "As much as he loves selling books, it's not nearly as exciting as his last profession." Camden snorts at the word "profession."

"He'd be back at that in a heartbeat if it wasn't for you, sweetie," Andrea says to Julia. "I saw him reading the paper yesterday, and when he came to the story about the burglary at Stern's Jewelers he got a faraway look in his eye, like a kid remembering a really good Christmas."

This alarms Julia, though she says nothing. She made clear to him early in their relationship that she would not be involved with a criminal, but he has never tested that and she has no idea if her resolve would hold if he did.

"Where is he anyway?" Camden asks. "He was supposed to check on the writer guy and come right back."

As if on cue, the front door opens and Sal and Max walk in. Actually, stumble in would be a better description, as they are both clearly drunk.

"You're drunk," Camden says, stunned. "How can you be drunk?"

"Easily, my dear," Max says. "The waitress kept bringing us drinks, and we drank them."

"Yes," Sal says. "We drank them. And I told my new friend of our plans for him, and he of his plans for me, for us. It was a meeting of the minds."

"I still cannot believe you're drunk," Camden says.

"I wouldn't agree with that assessment," Sal says defensively.

"Sal," Julia says. "Where were you the night of the Ithaca job?"

"Atlantic City," he answers immediately.

"Yep," she says with a nod. "You're drunk."

"We will plead to the lesser charge of semi-impairment," Max says. "Nothing a short nap, a shower, some coffee, and a steak won't cure."

"Right you are, Max" Sal says, clapping him on the shoulder. "First the nap. Wake us in two hours, no more, no less."

Before Camden can protest, they are up the stairs and gone.

"Looks like he found some excitement after all," Siren One says, then goes back to polishing her nails.

After the shop closes, much of the staff, including the almost-sober Sal and Max, gathers on the rooftop of the Dream Emporium, a popular restaurant and bar just down the street from The Last Word. Sal has convinced them to forego heading home in order to hear his grand plans and

Max's less grand literary idea. Max needs their cooperation much more than Sal needs his, though. Sal could find a writer willing to live at the store much easier than Max could find a new story idea.

Sal handles the introductions quickly, going around the several tables they have pushed together. He starts by introducing Max to the group, then the group to Max. Camden is there of course, as are Julia, Jacob, Heather, Ramon, Ben, and Siren One.

"Andrea," Camden corrects him.

"I don't mind, sweetie," she says. "Sal can call me anything he likes." Julia does not look pleased to hear this.

With the introductions out of the way, Sal moves on to the important stuff.

"Max has graciously agreed to become our first writer in residence," he proclaims proudly. They appear confused, except for Camden, who looks apprehensive, and Julia, who now smiles broadly. The idea has grown on her.

"What exactly is a writer in residence?" Heather asks. "I understand the concept as far as a university program, but we're a bookstore."

"It's really quite simple," Sal says. "Max will live with us at the store, help out occasionally, and work on his novel most of the time. I'll set up a workspace for him near the rare book room." He glances at Jacob, who is about to interrupt. "Near, Jacob," Sal clarifies. "Not inside." Jacob relaxes.

"Is he going to sleep in the store?" Ramon asks.

"No," Sal answers with a chuckle. "It would be cool if he could, but we're not set up for that. He will sleep in our apartment, unless he just has an urge to sleep on the floor downstairs."

"I've slept worse places," Max says flatly, which elicits nervous laughter from the group.

"How does this help us bring business into the store?" Ben asks. For a young sci-fi guy, he is very focused on the bottom line. Camden nods approvingly; she likes Ben, not just for his business focus but also because he is as handsome as a Greek god. Such a shame that he's gay, she thinks.

"By creating, or at least hopefully starting to create, a literary scene in this uncultured backwater," Sal responds. The word 'uncultured' sounds funny in his Jersey accent.

"We are not uncultured here," Julia interjects. "The arts are very strong in Fort Worth, you big goombah."

"I stand corrected," Sal concedes. "Literarily uncultured backwater." Julia nods.

"No offense to you, Mr. Luther," Ben says, clearly not buying Sal's explanation, "but how does one guy working on a novel in a corner of the store promote a literary movement here, or sales in the shop?"

"He can talk to customers," Julia says. "He can tell them what it's like to be a famous writer. People love that."

"Not so famous," Max says, reddening just a little. "And I wouldn't want to talk to people while I write. It's too hard to focus with all those interruptions."

Sal ponders this for a moment; he hadn't considered that obstacle.

"But," Max continues, "I could do something like what I did for a while when I lived in Brooklyn. I worked on the novel at my apartment or in coffee shops, but during part of the day I sat in front of a Greek restaurant with my old manual typewriter and wrote really short stories, no more than a couple pages, for five bucks each. I'd insert the person as a character and work in some small personal detail they gave me. People really liked it, and I got to where I could do four or five an hour, which didn't go far up there but wouldn't be bad here."

"What a cool idea," Heather says. "Did you sign them too?"

"Of course," Max replied. "For most of them that was the clincher. One lady from Phoenix convinced her husband to pay the five dollars by saying that a signed story would be worth a lot more than that when I was dead." *Which according to Wikipedia I am*, he thinks.

Heather turns to Camden. "We could have letterhead printed up with the store's name and logo, and he could use that instead of plain white paper. It would be great advertising, because people not only won't throw away a story written specifically for them, they will show it to their friends. Hell, they'll probably frame it."

Camden nods in agreement, and even Ben has no argument against it.

"Ok," Sal says. "We'll do it that way, and you can work on the novel in the apartment."

"I would probably use that coffee shop more often," Max says. "It's a nice place to write."

"I see the advertising benefit of the short stories," Ben persists. "But I still don't see how that moves the needle on people's interest in books, at least not by itself."

"That's why it is only phase one of the plan," Sal says. "Phase two is the Downtown Book Festival, presented by The Last Word and Crain Rare Books."

The table goes instantly silent; everyone stares at Sal wide-eyed except for Max, who doesn't understand the gravity of what Sal has just said.

"Crain Rare Books?" Jacob repeats, the first of them who is able to speak. Sal laughs, then shrugs.

"I suppose it does sound a little strange that we would work together on this."

"A *little* strange?" Jacob asks. "Given that you have twice pulled a gun on him, once after breaking into his home, I would call it more than a little strange."

"Has he actually agreed to partner with us on this?" Julia asks, as astonished as Jacob.

"He has," Sal replies. "I spoke with him about it this morning. I explained how it would benefit him and his store, and how bad it would look if he didn't participate."

"Ah," Camden says. "You threatened him again."

"Not at all," Sal says defensively. "And I am hurt that you assume that's the only way I can persuade people to do things."

"Are you sure?" she asks, unconvinced.

"Absolutely," he says firmly. "The fact is he needs publicity. If you think it's hard making ends meet with a general bookstore, try selling only rare and collectible stuff. Hell, ask Jacob."

Jacob nods in agreement. "I'm amazed he can still afford the rents down here. Unlike us, he doesn't own his building, and though when a valuable book sells it can bring in a lot of money, it can take an extraordinarily long time to sell a really valuable one."

"I don't see how publicity alone would sway him," Heather says, "given your past history with each other."

"We have reached a truce," Sal says. "He has agreed to be less of a pompous ass, and I have agreed to stop breaking into his home and threatening to shoot him. I have also been slowly buying back the books that Uncle Franklin sold him from his personal library, so he has a financial interest in me as well."

"It's still hard to believe that any of that was enough to convince him to work with *you*," Camden says.

"To be totally honest," Sal says with a mischievous grin, "there was one other inducement. Kim is going on a date with him tomorrow."

"Who is Kim?" Jacob asks.

"Siren Three," Camden replies. "I'm amazed Sal knows her name, but sadly not amazed that he is pimping out my employees."

"That's harsh," he says. "Besides, she asked me about him first. She apparently likes the nerdy bookish types."

"So when does this festival take place?" Ben asks. He sounds far less belligerent now, which given his imposing size is a good thing.

"In the spring," Julia says before Sal can respond. "It will take time and planning to do it the right way."

"Not like the Hemingway fiasco then." Ben says.

"It was not a fiasco," Sal retorts.

"Of course it wasn't," Julia says sweetly, patting his hand.

7

"Camden Makes Some Changes"

"Mr. Sal isn't going to like this," Ramon mutters as he removes a large stack of books from a shelf.

"Probably not," Julia agrees, setting her own smaller stack on an empty table. *In fact,* she thinks, *Sal is going to go ballistic, but maybe if he spent more time in the shop and less hanging out with his new drinking buddy author...* "Camden co-owns the place, Ramon, so she can make changes if she wants to."

Camden can't hear them, and likely wouldn't pay any attention if she could. She is too caught up in her new idea, busily restocking the newly-emptied shelves with brightly colored paperbacks, the front covers of which are all a variation on the same theme: a handsome, shirtless man embracing a flushed, full-figured woman about to burst out of her blouse/corset/bodice, a windswept castle in the background. It is the template for all romance novel covers.

"But the True Crime section?" Ramon continues, his voice a little louder. "Mr. Sal knows half of the people these were written about."

Julia suppresses a laugh, not wanting to offend Ramon, who is clearly quite serious about this.

"I don't think he knows any of the serial killers," she says. "Some of the bank robbers and a high percentage of the Mafia types, though."

"All for a bunch of romance novels? Really?"

"Yes, really," Camden says. She has walked up behind them without either realizing it. "I know you don't agree with this change," she continues, "but it's for the best. True Crime books simply don't sell, no matter how much Sal loves stocking them. People would rather watch that kind of thing on television than read about it."

Julia can't argue with this point; she is a Court TV addict herself. But that is really only half the argument.

"But romance novels?" she asks "That's not really something this store would normally carry."

Camden arches an eyebrow at her. "Have you forgotten how well *The Forbidden Fruit* sold last year?"

The Forbidden Fruit was the debut novel by an infamous English dominatrix that had taken the publishing world – though somehow not Camden – by surprise. It had been an international bestseller and had completely reshaped the erotica genre.

"No, I haven't forgotten," Julia answers. "I also haven't forgotten Sal's reaction when he saw we were stocking it. The two of you almost came to blows."

"Yet in the end I was proved right," Camden says smugly. "It made us a lot of money."

"But that was erotica," Julia persists, "not romance. There is a difference, in style, content and audience."

"There is indeed a difference," Camden agrees with a sharp nod of her head, "which is why we are going to have an erotica section as well."

Julia and Ramon stare at her, stunned. Julia starts to respond but Camden holds up her hand. "I don't expect Sal, or you Ramon, or any man for that matter, to understand why these genres even exist. Men are visual creatures, which is why half the Internet is devoted to pornography. Women are much more adept at *visualization*, which is quite different, and the reason romance is the top-selling genre in all of fiction, with erotica quickly gaining ground. Surely you understand that, Julia."

"I prefer my romance and erotica to be one-on-one, not in books," she replies without thinking. Ramon laughs uncomfortably; Camden says nothing. Julia imagines that she is "visualizing" her cousin and Julia, and quickly moves the conversation to safer territory. "Besides, the used bookstores and Blue Nile will kill our sales."

This takes Camden by surprise. "What?" she asks. "What do you mean they will kill our sales? How?"

"Simple logic," Julia says, "along with breaking down the sales data a little. Most people are going to buy erotica online from Blue Nile, partly because it can be hard to find in stores that don't have XXX in their name and peep shows in the back, and partly because the pastor's wife or head of the Junior League don't really want to hand that copy of *Amanda's Devilish Desires* to the salesperson at checkout."

"Ok, I can see your point there," Camden concedes. "But -"

"Women who read romance novels," Julia interrupts before she can protest, "tend to read a lot of them. But unlike a new hardcover mystery or one of the classics they don't tend to *keep* them. They swap them with friends or sell them to used bookstores so they can buy more."

Camden had to admit, if only to herself, that this was true. How often had she swapped romance novels with her girlfriends back in London?

"And just wait until that e-reader thing finally comes out this autumn," says a male voice. Camden turns to see Max Luther. He has come downstairs carrying his battered portable Royal typewriter, ready to begin a morning of writing stories for customer on the sidewalk in front of the shop.

"What do you mean?" Camden demands. There are entirely too many arguments popping up against her very good idea.

"The Kindle thing they keep talking about," Max says. "The one that's going to revolutionize how we read. Books without paper. I doubt it will ever replace real books, but it should be a big hit with the romance and erotica readers, which will decimate your sales."

"What makes you say that?" Camden asks.

"I overheard Julia's comment about ladies being embarrassed about people seeing them buying certain books," he explains. Julia likes the way he chose the word "ladies;" very courteous. "With an electronic reader they can buy anonymously online, and even read the stuff in public with no one knowing. It's gonna be a brave new world."

He nods, as much to himself as to any of them, and walks out the front door. Camden looks from the half-empty shelves to the half-full table, her mind racing. She had not considered any of these points, all of which are valid. The battle the change will cause with Sal can only be won with sales as her vindication, and now she is not sure she will be vindicated. Yet she is not one to back down either.

"You have made some good points," she announces finally. "Perhaps the prudent move, from a business perspective, would be a trail period on a smaller scale with a smaller selection. This would allow us to see how things go and also get the word out about the new offerings."

"So maybe we just reduce the True Crime section without totally eliminating it?" Julia suggests with a smile.

"Yes," Camden agrees. "That might be best."

"And maybe Sal won't notice for a while," Julia adds.

"That too."

8

"Spider Spin Me a Web"

The air is cool and crisp, the sun just breaking through some low clouds. It is a perfect day to be outside, a perfect day to write outside. Back home, Max thinks, it's probably sleeting already.

He nods a greeting at an elderly lady shuffling by on the sidewalk, matching the pace of an ancient Yorkshire terrier at the end of a purple leash. The dog had a purple sweater to match, and seems a little embarrassed about it. The lady smiles broadly at Max in return; he is clearly not in Brooklyn anymore.

Max sets the old Royal on a small oak table that Ramon has rescued from someone's garage sale. It might have been an attractive piece of furniture once, might even have qualified as an old-time writing desk. That was before a budding artist, or perhaps a drunken toddler, painted each of the legs a different, neon color: lime green, orange, sky blue, and pink. They had also carved some extremely impolite words into the tabletop, but his typewriter, papers, and coffee mug covered most of those.

Julia had very graciously made a sign with his name, the title of his most famous novel, and "Personalized Stories: $10.00;" the sign was securely taped to the front edge of the table. She felt five dollars was too little to ask for an original creation, and he liked her even more for that.

When he had done this in front of the Greek restaurant in Brooklyn he had been forced to use a small stool, similar to a drummer's throne, which had played havoc with his back. Here they had provided a straight-backed wooden chair that even had arms. He should have come South much sooner. He is still getting settled when the first person approaches him. It is actually a couple, but only the woman speaks.

"I've heard of you," she says in a tone that sounds slightly accusatory, as if he had ditched her on prom night or swindled her out of the family farm. "Ten dollars for a story? Seems cheap for a published author. I guess things aren't great for you."

He has no idea how to respond to this, so he simply looks at her husband – he had noticed the ring on the man's left hand – and raises an eyebrow. The man shrugs; this is his every day.

"This is simply a way for me to keep the creative juices flowing when I'm not working on my new novel," Max says, using one of many stock answers he gave; working in "creative juices" was key when talking to people who spent their lives in front of computers moving numbers in and out of spreadsheets.

"How long of a story?" she demands.

"Just a page or two," he answers, liking her less by the minute. "It's called flash fiction." It suddenly strikes him that while she is at least 40 years old, she is dressed like a teenager. The deep tan and dark roots flecked with gray, just visible under her blond mane, are evidence that she is clinging to her evaporating youth with a death grip. There is definitely a story in that.

"That seems short for ten dollars," she replies. "I expect you will sign it at least."

"Of course." Funny how many people think an author's signature is more valuable than the actual work he created. His signature wasn't even worth anything at the bottom of a check anymore.

"Fine," she says flatly, as if he has only barely met her requirements. "And how do I know you don't just have a template where the story is the same and you just insert my name into it?"

Spoken like a true user of Microsoft Word templates, he thinks. But it is actually a valid question, and something he had once considered doing back home. Only his artistic integrity and the fear of getting caught doing it prevented him.

"Easy," he says with as much of a smile as he can muster for this harpy. "You tell me the name and basic theme. I go from there."

She considers this for a long moment, and then turns toward her husband. "Ok," she says. "But write it about *him*."

Damn. There goes the whole Medusa angle.

The man steps forward, extending his hand; Max shakes it. His grip is a touch too soft.

"My name's Tony," he says.

"Ok, Tony," Max says, rolling a blank sheet of paper into the Royal. "Give me a theme."

"A theme?" Tony repeats. Max is sure the look on Tony's face is the same one from 8th grade when the teacher announced a pop quiz over the battles of the Revolutionary War.

"What would you like the story to be about? Max clarifies. "You know, a chance meeting, a heroic act, something criminal?"

Tony cuts his eyes over at his wife, then quickly back to Max. "Something criminal."

Max understands immediately; he would have given the same response if he were still married to Wife #2. He turns an idea around in his mind for several minutes, getting the structure straight in his head; the woman taps her foot impatiently. He settles on his story and begins typing, and his fingers fly across the keys. In a little under 15 minutes he is signing the bottom of the second of two pages. He hands them to Tony, who begins scanning the first page.

"Read it out loud," his wife says. "I'm paying for the thing after all."

Tony obediently begins reading aloud, the sound of the occasional car passing down Houston Street adding to the effect:

Deadly Questions

This was the one part of the job that I hated. But I had chosen this life and was happy with it. So I didn't complain. I wish I could have said the same for the woman sitting next to me.

"So where are we going?" she demanded.

"We've got to see Tommy B.," I answered.

"Why?"

"Because the Boss said so."

"I don't see why I had to come," she said, pouting like a small child. "I'm not one of his hired goons."

"I just do what I'm told," I replied like a good hired goon. "The boss said bring you, so I did."

She was silent for a moment, thank God. Lucy was one of those women who never shut up, which is what got her into the position she's in now. In our line of work you don't ask questions and you always keep your mouth shut, even if you're one of the boss's girlfriends. Especially if you're one of the boss's girlfriends. But she thought she knew everything and didn't hesitate to tell you.

"How far away is it?" Lucy asked.

"Not much farther," Tony answered from the back seat.

With Lucy's constant yammering I had almost forgotten Tony was in the car. It was never wise to forget about Tony, especially if he was behind you. Many had made that very mistake and paid dearly for it.

"Turn here," Tony said.

I turned off the two-lane blacktop onto a narrow gravel road. The sky was turning a bluish tint that you get right before the sun crests the horizon. The gravel made the car vibrate slightly, which was not to my liking. A smooth ride was better for this.

"Who the hell would live out here?" Lucy asked in a huff. It was easy to be condescending about others' lot in life when yours was so comfortable.

"I told you," I said, "Tommy B. lives out here." It was getting harder for me to remain polite.

"This is stupid," she replied. "Why did I have to get up before dawn to come see some guy in the sticks?"

Out of the corner of my eye I can see Tony's arm moving up. Lucy doesn't see anything; she's too busy asking the wrong questions.

"I should have hooked up with old man Vario," she continued. "He treats his girlfriends like princesses, even better than his wife. Do you think he would send his best girl out to the sticks at five in the morn..."

The bullet stopped her incessant talking in mid-sentence. She slumped forward, her head resting against the dash. The faint smell of gunpowder filled the car. I pulled over into a shallow ditch.

"I wonder if that answered her question?" Tony asked.

Tony, the real-life one, looked up after he finished reading. His smile was wide; his wife's was not.

"You call that a story?" she huffs, clearly missing the not-so-hidden meaning. "I'm not paying for that. You can if you want to throw away ten dollars, but I am most certainly not. She headed up the sidewalk without another word.

Tony pulls a twenty dollar bill from his wallet and hands it to Max. "Keep the change," he says, then follows his wife, happily clutching the pages of his story.

Max writes five more stories that morning before heading off to lunch with Sal, but none was as gratifying, for either him or the readers, as the one where Tony finally got the last word.

9

"Hurricane Alice"

"I demand to see Salvatore Terranova."

Julia's head snaps up in alarm, but she relaxes immediately when she sees the voice belongs to neither a cop nor a mob hit man. It belongs, in fact, to an older woman in her mid-60s; her silver hair is cut in a bob and she is dressed as if ready for a business meeting. Julia has never seen her before, but there is something familiar about the woman, especially the eyes. Before she can speak, Camden does.

"Aunt Alice?" she exclaims, moving quickly around the counter.

"Camden," the woman replies, her tone softening only slightly.

"It's been so long since I've seen you," Camden says. "You look wonderful."

Alice nods, whether in appreciation or simple agreement Julia cannot tell. She does notice that they do not hug or even shake hands, which she finds odd. They simply stare at each other while Julia does some quick genealogical calculations.

Camden's mother is English, and this woman has no accent; her father was George Templeton, the brother of the late Franklin Templeton, from whom Sal and Camden inherited the bookstore. Franklin only had two siblings: Camden's father and a younger sister who is –.

"Hello ma," Sal says at the exact moment Julia realizes who she is. The woman turns slowly around to face him and Julia see, for just a split second, affection in her eyes. The earlier fury returns immediately.

"Do not 'hello ma' me, Salvatore," she says coldly. "You disappear without a trace more than a year ago, no call, no note. I was convinced those people you associate with had done something awful to you and that you were probably buried somewhere in the Pine Barrens."

Sal stares at his mother, amazed. He is not even sure how to begin to answer this insanity. To make matters worse, Julia and Camden are staring at him like he is the worst son to ever walk the planet.

"Ma," he says as calmly as he can, "I came to your house the day I left. I told you Uncle Franklin had died and asked you to come to the funeral. You said your canasta group was meeting that night and that you couldn't cancel on such short notice. Then you said to call if he left you anything and mumbled something about him and his stupid books and went back to watching *Days of Our Lives*."

Cam and Julia look to Alice now, who is as defiant as before.

"And did the old fool leave me anything?" she asks.

"No, ma," Sal says. "I called and told you that he left the store to Camden and me and that I would be staying down here."

"I don't remember that at all."

"Yeah, well I made the mistake of calling the night of your mah-jongg group and you were already half-lit by that point."

"I do not get half-lit," she says firmly. "I have the occasional glass of wine, for my health."

"And the frequent whisky sour," he retorts. "Your last words to me were 'you are a dago bum just like your worthless father, God rest his soul.' Then you hung up. So you really shouldn't be shocked that I didn't send a Christmas card."

By this point everyone in the store, customers and staff alike, are staring at them. Camden suggests they go upstairs where they can talk in private, and she will make them all some tea.

"This is a sweet girl who knows how to treat her elders," Alice says. "I should have married an Englishman instead of an Italian."

"Worked out great for Cam," Sal snickers. Camden tries to hit him, but fails.

"Yes, I definitely should have stayed away from the Italians," Alice continues as they head for the stairs, more to herself than them. "But he looked so handsome in that Brooks Brothers suit standing outside the Waldorf Astoria on New Year's Eve…" Her words trail off, but once again Julia senses affection in them, if only briefly. And it looks like she will finally get to meet her boyfriend's mother.

Alice is seated at the kitchen table, waiting patiently as Camden pours tea and Sal puts chocolate biscuits – the English kind – on a plate. As he passes Camden he whispers "You see why Franklin left nothing to his little sister?"

"I heard that Salvatore," Alice says. "No respect at all. Camden dear, could you splash a little Baileys in the tea?"

Sal answers for her. "It's tea, ma. You put Baileys in coffee."

"Oh," Alice says, disappointed. "Then I'll take a small glass on the side if you don't mind."

Camden has no clue how to respond to this, but to Sal it is clearly nothing new. He takes down a bottle of Baileys Irish Cream and fills a juice glass halfway. He then takes the tea from Cam and sets both down in front of his mother.

"Tea with a Baileys chaser, Mrs. Terranova," he says. "Or as I called it growing up: breakfast."

Alice ignores him, taking a sip of the Baileys and a bite of a biscuit. She ignores the tea. Sal takes a seat across the table from his mother, choosing a Sam Adams over tea; Camden sits with them and tries to move the conversation to more pleasant ground.

"What brings you down here after so long, Aunt Alice?" she asks.

"Paulie stopped by to see me last week," she says. Camden does not know who Paulie is, but Sal grimaces, which Alice notices. "Yes, Paulie," she says to Sal. "Only your best friend since third grade whom you haven't spoken to in months. He still checks on me occasionally, like a *good* son would. Why have you not called him, Salvatore?"

Sal sighs and downs half of the beer in one long swig.

"Because every time we talk he has some new scheme he wants me to go in on with him. I've told him a hundred times that I'm out of that business, but he won't listen."

"He is simply trying to provide for his family in tough economic times," Alice says.

Sal is taking another swig as she says this, and he nearly spits it out.

"What? Provide for his family? You always said I was a no-good criminal that brought shame to your historic

95

Templeton name, but Paulie's simply providing for his family?"

"You were always so flashy about it," Alice says with a disapproving shake of her head. "Doing those high-profile heists and leaving books behind to taunt the police...so rude. Paulie is much more discreet." She finishes off the Baileys and hands the glass across to Sal. "Another one, please, and don't be so stingy with it this time."

He gets up and refills the glass, staring at the Drano by the sink with evil thoughts as he does, then sets the glass down by the untouched tea.

"I thought you would be happy that your son has a legitimate career now," Camden says, hoping to pull at least one positive word out of her aunt.

"Legitimate?" Alice laughs; her laugh is surprisingly hearty and infectious. "If you call poverty legitimate. There is no money in selling books, everyone knows that."

"We've done alright," Sal says defensively.

"I don't understand," Camden persists. "You would rather he be a criminal than a bookseller?"

"I would rather he be able to provide for his mother in her golden years. I wanted him to be a doctor or a lawyer, but he wanted to be just like that father of his. Even though he knew he could never be a made man."

"Why not?" Camden asks. Her knowledge of the Mafia is confined to a few movies and the little Sal has told her.

"Remember Henry Hill in *Goodfellas*?" he asks. She stares blankly at him. "Ray Liotta played him." She remembers and nods. "Right, well I had the same glaring problem he did, and it was *her* fault."

"I'm still confused," Camden says.

"He's only half Italian," Alice explains. "To listen to him you'd think that he was full Italian going back to the time of the Caesars, but he's not. His father was Italian, but as you know we Templetons are English and Scottish, so he could never be made, never be a full member of a crew. He could only be an associate."

Sal glares at her when she says "associate." This is still a sore subject with him. But now Camden is curious, since Sal rarely speaks about his old life except for a few funny stories.

"Was your father a made man?" she asks. Before he can answer Alice jumps in.

"He was for about thirty minutes," she says. "He waits half his life for it, does two stretches in Attica, and right after the ceremony they go to Atlantic City and he has a heart attack when his roulette number hits."

"Yeah," Sal says bitterly, "and all you cared about was that the casino wouldn't give you his winnings."

He stands and storms out of the apartment without another word; Alice smiles at Camden and calmly sips her Baileys.

When Sal returns to the shop several hours later, Camden is back behind the counter bagging up a customer's purchases. He quickly scans the store; his mother is nowhere in sight.

"Where is she?" he asks Camden after the customer departs.

"She went back to her hotel. She's staying at the Belmont just up the street."

"Lovely. Any clue when she might be going home?"

"She didn't say, but Julia talked to her before she left and I think the three of you are having dinner tonight."

"We are not," Sal says.

"Sure we are," Julia says as she walks up to the counter. "It will be fun."

Camden wonders if Julia would have asked Alice to dinner if she had been upstairs to hear the conversation she heard. It will be a lot of things, but fun is not one of them.

"Besides," Julia continues, "fun or not, at least one of us will have finally met the other's parents."

Her tone is a few degrees colder than icy, and Sal knows better than to respond. He briefly considers asking if meeting her parents tonight instead is an option, but guesses that this will not be well received. Best to just change the subject.

"How was she after I left?" he asks Camden.

"About the same, just with more Baileys. We need another bottle, by the way. She finished it."

"Wonderful. What does about the same mean exactly?"

Camden ponders this question for longer than Sal likes.

"I'm not completely sure," she finally admits. "At first it sounded like she wanted something, like money or something like that. But after the fourth glass of Baileys it seemed more like she missed you and just wanted to see you."

"She gets sentimental when she's loaded," he says. "Of course, you have to make it past mean, vindictive, and impossible to please in order to reach sentimental, and I rarely stuck around that long. Pop was better at it than me."

"Maybe she's sick and wants to make peace with you before something happens," Julia suggests, ever the peacemaker.

"She'll never die," Sal says. "God won't have her, and the Devil is afraid she'd be running Hell within a week of getting there."

"I thought good Italian Catholic boys loved their mothers," Julia says. Sal's shoulders slump, which shock her.

"I do love her," he says softly. "I always have, no matter what happened. She just makes it so damn hard..." He is silent for a moment, and then recovers. "What time is dinner?"

"7:30," Julia says.

"That gives me time to buy another bottle of Baileys and finish it off before we go," he says, heading for the door again. "Fight drunk with drunk, I always say."

For reasons Sal cannot fathom, Julia has agreed that they will meet Alice for dinner at the restaurant inside the Belmont Hotel. He isn't sure how his mother can afford a room there, but he is sure that the overpriced and innocuously named Schooners Bistro will set him back at least a couple hundred dollars. When they arrive, Alice is already seated at a table in the center of the restaurant, a half-empty bottle of wine beside her. Sal is no aficionado, but he is sure the bottle was not cheap. He glares at Julia, who smiles back.

They make the usual small talk as Sal mentally calculates the cost of what everyone is ordering, plus the wine. When he is finished he realizes that fancy restaurants rob people far more efficiently than the mob ever did. After the waiter sets down a plate of fried mozzarella and Alice orders another bottle of wine, she turns to Julia with the sweetest smile Sal has ever seen crease his mother's face.

"I am so glad Salvatore found a nice girl down here," she says. Julia beams. "Not like those floozies he used to go around with." Julia's smile fades. "And it fits nicely with the reason I'm here."

Sal tenses visibly. *Here it comes,* he thinks.

"I'm getting married!" Alice exclaims in much the same way a game show host announces that you have just won a new car. Several nearby diners turn to look at them, and Sal understands why she chose a table in the middle of the restaurant. Alice Templeton Terranova loves being the center of attention.

"That's wonderful," Julia gushes, squeezing Alice's hand. Sal notices his mother flinch slightly; she is not fond of physical contact, but the moment requires that she accept it.

"Who's the lucky guy," Sal forces himself to ask, relieved that at least she isn't here to ask him for money.

"Carmine Delvecchio," she says, her voice much softer now.

"Carmine Delvecchio?" Sal repeats. "From next door? The Carmine Delvecchio dad bowled with for years? The one whose wife used to babysit me when I was a kid, the one you always said was just another wop with no ambition? *That* Carmine Delvecchio?" He does not realize that his voice has been steadily rising with each question, or that people are now staring at him rather than his mother. Julia stares at him, alarmed.

"Yes," Alice says defiantly. "And he is a good man, at least a better man now than he was. Carmela died a few years back, and we started talking more and more and last month he popped the question. We're going to sell both houses and move to Coral Cables near his sister and nephews."

Sal's shock has subsided, and after a moment he no longer feels outraged that his mother would marry one of Pop's friends. Now he feels sorry for Carmine.

"That's just great, ma," he says with as much sincerity as he can muster. "I hope you'll both be very happy in Florida. Sure as heck beats Jersey." And absolutely beat her living in Texas; at least Florida is still four states away.

"Thank you," she says as she cuts into the filet mignon the waiter has just placed in front of her. "And of course you will be the one to give me away."

He had not expected this, hadn't even considered the possibility of it, but to refuse would make him look like a heartless bastard to Julia, so he simply nods.

"And if you could see fit to use part of the money from that Ithaca heist for the down payment on our condo –"

"I knew it," he says through gritted teeth. "There is no money, and even if there was you and Carmine would never see a penny of it."

"Of course there's money," Alice replies, ignoring the second part of his statement. "Everyone knows that, even Paulie. He's the one who suggested I ask you."

It all made sense now. Paulie was pissed at Sal's refusal to go in with him on any new jobs, and had taken his revenge by setting Alice on him. He would pay dearly for this.

"That job wasn't really what everyone thinks," Julia says. "If Sal had been there," she adds quickly, glancing at him. "Which he wasn't." He gives her a quick wink.

"Of course it was dear," Alice replies condescendingly. "He's just like his father. He always claimed to have no money too, but somehow he could always afford to bet on the horses, the greyhounds, and the Jets. Don't make the same mistake I did; get out while you can."

"The only mistake you made was coming here," Sal says, standing up and pulling Julia to her feet. He tosses three one hundred dollar bills on the table. "Good to see ma, as always. Keep whatever's left after the tip as a wedding present, and see if Paulie can give you away. I'll be busy that weekend. Have a safe trip back to Trenton."

Julia is silent on the walk back to Sal's place. It had gone about as badly as was possible, and she is sure that he will never want to meet her parents now. With that woman as an example his whole life, who could blame him for not being keen on marriage?

In what has become an eerily regular occurrence, Sal guesses what she's thinking. "Are there books in your parents' house," he asks. The question catches her off guard with its apparent randomness.

"Of course," she replies. "In fact, my dad converted my old bedroom into his library when I moved out. With three kids he never had room for one before."

"Good," Sal says. "Because there were none in my house that weren't mine, and I'm sure there are none now. It tells you a lot about person, having books in the house."

"It does," she agrees."

"I guess I should meet them sometime to see what a normal family looks like."

"Normal might be a strong word," she says.

"Compared to what you just suffered though?" he asks. "That was my every night for 17 years."

"When you put it that way," she says, "then yes, mine is pretty normal compared to that."

"Thought so," he replies. "We never really ate, even though it cost me three bills. How about some pizza?"

"Sounds great," she says, slipping her hand into his. In spite of everything that's happened today, she thinks, the night is ending on a wonderful note. Maybe Hurricane Alice blowing into town was a good thing after all.

10

"The Matchmaker"

Perhaps it is how well things went with Sal the night before that causes Julia to do something she would otherwise never do: play matchmaker. For some time now Luis' friend Jake has been coming into the store, browsing around a bit, but only staying if he sees that Heather is working. There is obvious chemistry between them (though she thinks Heather probably has enough chemistry for two people by herself), but he never seems to take the initiative. And to her surprise, other than a few not so subtle hints, Heather doesn't either.

Julia is aware that Jake has a girlfriend or fiancé or something; she has even seen her in the store a few times with Jake, always complaining either that they don't have enough study Bibles or that what they do have is somehow demonic. But according to Ortiz, Jake would love nothing more than to be rid of her; he simply has yet to find a good way to tell her. Men are such idiots sometimes; the only good way to tell her is to tell her.

She would not really care much about Jake's interest in Heather; he's not her friend and doesn't hang out with Sal. But she does care about Heather's interest in him. She was initially more than a little threatened when Heather was first hired, both because Cam and Sal had both liked her most of all the new applicants and because she openly flirted with Sal every chance she got.

Sal, to her relief and amazement, had been far more taken with her than he was with Heather, and to Heather's credit the flirting had stopped once that became clear. And while Heather was still closer to Camden (they went to the midnight screening of *The Rocky Horror Picture Show* nearly every Friday), they had bonded during a girls' weekend last spring over the least likely of subjects: 1980s alternative music. Since then there had been many times after work where they had jumped in Heather's car and spent the entire evening driving the long circle of Loop 820 listening to the Violent Femmes, the Cure, Depeche Mode, and the Psychedelic Furs. Heather's personal favorite was, unsurprisingly, the Smiths, while Julia was more partial to the Replacements.

This shared love of a long-vanished genre of music was not enough to make them close friends by itself, but when combined with working together daily and an obvious love for books it had been the catalyst that moved them in that direction. It bothered Julia that in spite of her intelligence, sense of humor, and outward confidence, Heather often ended up with guys that were lazy, freeloaders, trouble, or some combination of the three. She didn't know a lot about Jake, and he might well be trouble (he was Ortiz' best friend after all), but he was certainly neither lazy nor a freeloader.

This is all on Julia's mind when the man himself walks into the store, looks around for a minute, sees Heather setting up yet another Hemingway display, and moves quietly to the fiction section. She watches with increasing amusement as Jake and Heather try to watch each other without the other noticing. Surely this guy didn't hesitate this long before taking a shot back when he was an Army sniper; he'd be dead now if that were the case.

Julia walks up to him as he is scanning the back cover of David Foster Wallace's *Infinite Jest*. He looks up quickly when he hears her, probably thinking she is Heather.

"Thinking about getting that one?" she asks. "You're brave if you do. I've never been able to finish it."

"I look at it every time I come in," he says. "It's my next big 'literary' project. Took four years to finally finish *Ulysses*, but I managed, so I think I can eventually defeat this one."

He smiles when he says this, and Julia can immediately see why Heather is attracted to him; he has a great smile. She knows he is at least 10 years older than Heather, probably more than that, but he is in excellent shape, keeps his hair close-cropped, and exudes a confident air.

"You like a challenge?" she asks. "I have one for you."

He gives her a puzzled look.

"Here it is," she says, lowering her voice. "You can keep coming in here pretending to browse our shelves while actually stealing glances at my friend over there until you're both old and gray, or you can ask her out."

"Is it that obvious?" he asks. To her surprise the smile does not vanish.

"Only to everyone who works here, most of the customers, the mailman, and the UPS guy."

"And to Heather as well, I guess," he says. This time the smile does fade a bit.

"Yes," Julia says, "to her as well. But everyone also notices that when you come in she isn't really working on a display or whatever; she's stealing glances at you."

"So what do you suggest?" he asks. "Just go up and ask her out? My situation is a little...complicated."

"So is she," Julia replies. "Come with me."

They walk over to the table where Heather is exchanging copies of *Death in the Afternoon* for copies of *A Farewell to Arms*. She does a fairly good job of acting like she doesn't see them until Julia speaks.

"Heather," she says, "can you convince Jake to quit procrastinating and just buy this copy of *Infinite Jest* already?"

Heather arches an eyebrow, which makes the small silver bar that runs through it lift as well. Jake continues smiling.

"It's a great book," she says. "I've read it twice. You should definitely get it."

"Ok," he says. Julia doubts he has heard any of what either of them said. He would have agreed if she had suggested he juggle flaming chainsaws.

"Cool," Julia says, taking the book from him. "Oh, by the way Jake, Sal and Heather and I are going for coffee after work tonight. Since Heather and I will be talking girl stuff most of the time, I'm sure Sal would appreciate having a guy there to talk to. Why don't you join us?"

Jake blinks rapidly a few times, having not expected this at all. To her credit, Heather shows no surprise at all.

"Sounds great," he says, recovering his composure. "It will be a nice change from always listening to Luis' plans for world domination."

"Awesome. We'll meet up at The Daily Grind at 6:30. Now let me ring up that book for you."

She leads him back to the counter, runs his credit card, and hands him back the book. He gives her a grateful smile, which she acknowledges with a nod, and then leaves the store. The second the door closes Heather rushes over to her and before Julia knows what is happening she has enveloped her in a bear hug.

"You are *so* my best friend ever!" she exclaims. "Such quick thinking, such calm delivery; you should be an actress. But are you sure Sal wants me – and now Jake – tagging along on your date?"

"You're not," Julia replies with a wicked grin. "Sal and I are both here until 9:00 tonight."

"But you just invited me, us, to go with you."

"Yeah, sorry about the mix-up," Julia says. "I guess it's just going to be the two of you." She starts to laugh, but can't: Heather is once again squeezing all the air out of her in a massive embrace. The girl is a lot stronger than she looks.

The Daily Grind is busy at 6:30, but Jake had arrived early and secured four overstuffed chairs, just beating out some bearded grad students. They started to protest, but his glare convinced them that a table would suit them fine. At 6:35, Heather walks in, sees him, and takes one of the empty chairs.

"What can I get you?" he asks. "Or should we wait for Sal and Julia?"

"I'll take a vanilla latte," she says. "And it turns out that Sal and Julia have to work late, so it's just us tonight."

Julia, he thinks. That girl is smooth.

When he returns with their coffee two of the grad students are seated in the chairs he had saved for Sal and Julia. They quickly rise when he walks over.

"She said it was okay," one stammers, motioning to Heather.

"Sure, sure," Jake says, motioning for the kid to sit back down. He places their coffee on the small table that barely separates their two chairs, searching frantically for some way to start the conversation. He thinks back to the night they first met, at a book signing at the store.

"So did you ever read *The Razor's Edge*?" he finally asks after taking a sip of his coffee. Plain Americano, black; none of that silly no-fat-no-whip-soy-three-pump-vanilla-latte crap for him.

"Yes," Heather says. "Right after you recommended it." Her coffee is almost one of the 'no-this' kind, but he's not going to judge her.

"Did you like it?"

"I did. I especially liked the way Maugham inserted himself in the story as a semi-narrator. I wish Papa would have done that in one of his novels."

"I've noticed your Hemingway fixation," he replies. "Don't you think he actually did insert himself in every book, as the main character no less?"

"I suppose you're right," she says with a laugh. She has a great laugh. "What do you like most about it? The search for meaning thing?"

"Sure," he says, "that part's interesting enough. But I get something new from it every time I read it, which is once a year every year since '86."

"I was an infant in '86," she says with a grin. For a moment Jake is speechless, but he recovers and continues.

"What I found most interesting with this last reading is how similar the events are to what we're going through today. War, financial crisis, guys coming back from combat with few prospects, wondering what it all means."

"I noticed that too," Heather agrees. "Of course they're coming back to Topeka and Tulsa and Flagstaff, while Larry got to go to Paris. One advantage of a European war, I guess."

"Yeah, hanging around Baghdad or Kabul wouldn't be nearly as much fun."

"I really liked Isabel," Heather says. This shocks him.

"She wasn't very likeable," he says. "In fact, she bordered on evil by the end."

"I don't agree at all," Heather argues. "She knew what she wanted and did what she had to do in order to get it."

"But in the end she didn't get what she wanted."

"Sure she did. She just had to adjust what she wanted to fit her new reality."

"That is a very interesting way of looking at it. Twisted, but interesting."

"I have a very unique worldview," she says proudly.

The only view Jake has at the moment is of her legs. She is wearing a black knit shirt and a very short khaki skirt with black boots, and he has to force himself to look back at her face. She catches this and grins again.

"Right," he says quickly. "Worldview."

"I can sum it up for you in just a few lines," she says. "But you're a preacher, and I don't want to offend you."

"I'm not easily offended," he says.

"Ok. It's a saying from a very famous Bodhisattva…that's a Buddha –"

"Who forsakes Nirvana and returns to earth to lead others to enlightenment," he finishes. She stares, open-mouthed. "Christianity isn't the only religion I know a few things about."

"Impressive," she says with an approving nod. "So let me write it down and you can tell me what you think." She pulls a pen from her purse, quickly scribbles some lines on a napkin, and hands it to him.

The napkin is completely covered with her surprisingly neat handwriting, and it looks like a poem of some kind, or maybe a Zen koan. It talks about the world being wicked, light in the darkness, lost hope, and the need for peace and love and understanding. He looks up when he finishes, and for a moment isn't sure if she's joking.

"This is an Elvis Costello song," he says.

"Okay," she says with a smile, "maybe he's not a Bodhisattva. But he is famous. And it sounds like something the Buddha would agree with."

He laughs, and realizes he hasn't truly enjoyed a woman's company this much since before he and Amy got engaged. At which point she adds mind reader to her list of attributes.

"So does the blonde Amazon know you're here semi-flirting with me?" she asks.

"Say again?" he says, taken aback.

"You know, the tall blonde with the store-bought tan who was with you at the store the first time we met. The one who thinks Eastern religions are of the devil. She's your fiancé, right?"

"How did you know that?"

"Ortiz talks to me, too," she says with a twinkle in her eye. "So, does she know?"

"No," he says, "but she doesn't get a vote."

"I won't tell if you don't," she says, her voice suddenly low and husky. "How did you end up with her anyway? She doesn't seem like your type, if you don't mind me saying."

He doesn't mind at all, and has asked himself the same question many times, though he's not sure how Heather would have any clue what his type was.

"If you really want to hear the story I'll give you the thumbnail version," he says, and she nods. "Ok. Amy Sanders is the daughter of an immensely well-respected pastor; by her own account she became a Christian as soon as she was old enough to toddle down the church aisle.

"When she was graduating from Baylor, I was still running around the world making people that Uncle Sam didn't like disappear. I had lost my wife to a car accident years before —" he pauses here, and Heather, who had no idea, puts her hand over his.

"You don't have to tell me all this if you don't want to," she says, though she really does want to hear it.

"Nah, I'm fine," he says. "Anyway, after Lori died I fell into a period of heavy drinking and poor decisions before pulling my head out of my ass. Then I met Amy; she set her sights on me at a Missions Conference I was speaking at and I didn't stand a chance.

"She wasn't there to learn about missions, of course. She was part of the church's Communications Team and was passing out binders of information. She saw that as her contribution to the cause of world evangelism. Not that my motives were completely pure; I got into missions initially because I was used to being in foreign countries."

"Sounds like as good a reason as any," Heather says with a laugh.

"I suppose," he says. "Amy turned on the charm that day, and I was hooked. We were engaged before I realized she had any flaws, let alone that she had so many. It's a little embarrassing to admit this, but we got engaged so fast because she informed me there would be no sex until there was at least the promise of marriage; we both obviously had strong Christian morals."

"I'm a Methodist," she says. "We don't have as many restrictions on that kind of thing."

"You told the nun that day that you're a Wiccan," Jake replies.

"See?" she says. "Apparently I lie too. Scandalous." Before he can decide if she's joking, she hits him with another surprising question. "So was the sex worth it?"

"Not really," he answers.

"Why don't you just call it off?" she asks.

"It's complicated," he says.

"Hmmm…complicated. I'm thinking that it's a combination two things," she says.

"Really? And what would those be?"

"First, you said her dad was a big-time preacher. If you kick his daughter to the curb it probably hurts your preachy business thing too."

"Probably," he says, laughing at how she describes his vocation.

"Second, you've probably tried to talk about it with her, with no luck. The little you've said makes her sound like someone who's always gotten her way. I bet if you bring up any subject she doesn't like she starts crying, and as a man you have no clue how to deal with that. It's our secret weapon."

"Yeah," he admits, "she does that sometimes. And sometimes she goes on the offensive and hits me with some really brutal lines."

"I love brutal lines!" she exclaims. "Tell me one; maybe I can use it sometime. Not on you of course."

"Of course. The best one so far is 'everyone who loves me hates you.' I mean, how do you respond to that?"

"Killer," Heather says admiringly. "I wouldn't have thought Miss Country Club had it in her."

"Enough about me and my screwed up life," Jake says. "Tell me about you."

"No," she says.

"What? Why not?"

"Tonight happened because my friend took the initiative for both of us," she says, her tone suddenly very professional. "And in spite of our mutual attraction – don't give me that look, we both know there is mutual attraction – in spite of that, I needed to know where things stand with you and the preacher's daughter. Now I do."

"And now you don't want to talk anymore?" he asks.

"No, I do, definitely. But to get my story you have to call me and ask me out on a real date."

Jake tries to think of a good argument against this line of reasoning, but he can't.

"I don't have your number," is all he can say.

She takes back the napkin with the Costello koan, writes a ten-digit number at the bottom, and hands it to him. "Let's have dinner sometime. Soon."

He looks at the napkin, then back at her.

"I thought the new thing was for you to just put your number in my cell phone," he says with a smirk.

She leans across the table, and in the process a gap opens at the top of her shirt; tattooed above her left breast are the eyes from the cover artwork of *The Great Gatsby*. She puts her lips close to his ear, and in that same low, husky voice says "I guess I'm just an old-fashioned girl." She gives him a quick kiss on the cheek, downs the remainder of her latte, and is gone before he can say another word.

11

"Girls, Girls, Girls"

When Jake gets back to his loft, Amy is sitting on the couch reading a magazine. Clearly he either needs to change the locks or stop giving his key to everyone he knows. Of course, she is his fiancé, technically speaking. He nods a greeting, grabs a bottled water from the fridge, and sits down beside her.

"You never call me anymore," she says. "First you're gone all the time, and now you don't even call."

"I've got a lot going on right now," he says. He is the master of understatement.

"My dad tells me that you're in some kind of trouble with the denomination. Something about quoting some columnist in your sermon."

"He probably said communist, not columnist," he replies, "and it was actually a Brazilian priest." Normally he would have found this error amusing, but tonight it just makes him feel more tired. The quote had been by Dom Helder Camara: *"When I give food to the poor, they call me a saint. When I ask why the poor have no food, they call me a communist."* Seemed fairly biblical when he said it.

"Oh," she says. "That makes more sense. I can see why they'd be mad about that. Why don't you just apologize?"

"Why should I apologize?"

"Come on now, Jake. You can't go around quoting communists, or priests for that matter. The next thing I know you'll be telling people you're a Democrat."

He suddenly moves from tired to exhausted. All he wants now is for her to go away so he can get some sleep. So he asks her to leave.

"You're kidding, right?" she asks, amazed.

"No. I'm tired."

"Then don't let me keep you up," she says, standing and moving toward the door.

As she slams it behind her she remarks that she cannot believe what a complete asshole he is. It pretty much crystallizes what he once liked and now could not stand about her: behind the pretty face and great body, she was a loud, hard-drinking, narrow-minded preacher's daughter. He would change the locks in the morning.

The rain falls in stiff, gray sheets, and distant thunder promises more to come. The canopy covering the rooftop bar protects them from the brunt of the storm, with only those latecomers who are consigned to the western edge of the covering getting wet. They don't appear to mind, and in any case the club will only close the roof area if lightning becomes a threat.

The view of downtown Ft. Worth at night is impressive, though nowhere near as famous as many other cities in America. On this night, however, much of the male attention on the roof is focused on Heather, who is there with Jake; she is wearing a mesh tank top and a skirt that Jake had initially mistaken for a wide belt. Heather, Julia and Camden are in deep in conversation with Luis, which is always an adventure in itself. Sal and Jake return with fresh beers in time to pick up the conversation the ladies are having with Luis.

"So your father was a Sergeant-Major?" Julia asks. "Did you join the Army because it was a family tradition?" He smiles that big smile of his that always put people at ease, sometimes to their eventual regret.

"Nothing like that," Luis says. "I had a little trouble one night in Miami, and it was a choice of four years with the Green Machine or four years on the farm in Dade County."

She looks at him, confused.

"A join the Army or go to jail kind of choice," Sal whispers. She nods.

"A simple choice, really," Luis says.

Camden shows no hint of being concerned about his youthful indiscretions; she just snuggles closer to him. This surprises Sal; his cousin is such a straight arrow in all things except as they relate to Ortiz.

"But you stayed longer than four years," Julia continues. "So you must have liked the life."

"I liked my bro here," he says, motioning to Jake. "When we got teamed up in sniper school, I knew they'd keep us together, and we had a hell of a lot of fun."

"Jake has told me a little about some of your fun," Heather says with a grin. "But oddly enough, he never mentions women. Were you two monks or just closet lovers?"

Jake spits out the beer he was about to swallow, and Luis flushes crimson for a split second.

"I will overlook that statement this time," he says. "Of course there were women. Only after Lori had passed of course, God rest her soul." He crossed himself as he said this. "He had a terrible weakness for the Latin beauties."

Jake does not like where this is going and takes the opportunity to interrupt.

"But I've been cured of that," he says. "I have been converted to girls with a fondness for ink and a Hemingway fetish."

"A good choice as well," Ortiz replies with a nod. "But the English, the English were sent by God himself." Camden giggles like a teenager at this, and Sal rolls his eyes. Julia sees this and elbows him in the ribs.

"So you two have been together since you were teenagers," Julia says to Jake.

"Yep, a very long time," he answers.

"Kind of like Batman and Robin?" Heather says.

He winces at the comparison, and is sure that Lou will dismiss her from their presence immediately, but he only smiles. She is, after all, still quite young.

"No, my dear," he says sweetly. "Batman and Robin have an unequal relationship, by which I mean Robin brings nothing to the table. He is a foil, a sidekick. A better comparisons would be Butch and Sundance, Vito Corleone and Clemenza…"

"Bruce and Clarence," Sal interjects.

"The most apt comparison would be Spenser and Hawk," Luis finishes, "though you may not have heard of them."

"Those are equal then?" Camden asks.

"Yes," Ortiz says. "In each example they could exist quite well separately, but are much more effective together."

"Yet you seem to follow his lead," Julia observes. It is not a question.

"Of course. Someone has to lead, and Jake has the one quality that I – like Sundance, Clemenza, and The Big Man – often lack: discipline." He smiles broadly.

"What about this Hawk person?" Camden asks. "Does he lack discipline as well?"

"No," Jake answers, "and neither does Luis, no matter what he may tell you."

"So how did you end up in the ministry with him?" Julia asks Luis, changing the subject.

"I am technically not in the ministry with him," Luis explains. "I function as more of a business manager and consultant of sorts. I leave the religious aspect totally to him."

"In other words he gives you a legitimate source of income, one you can pay taxes on," Sal says.

"It is so pleasant to have someone around who grasps the difficulties I face," Luis replies happily. "Salvatore understands that the powers that be frown upon a man not having a traceable, taxable source of income. My brother Jake provides this for me, and in exchange I perform the occasional service for him."

"What kind of service?" Heather asks.

"Just this week I had to kill three Jehovah's Witnesses who were muscling in on his soul-winning territory," Luis says, shaking his head sadly. He then starts whistling "All Along the Watchtower," but only Jake gets it.

Julia gasps and Heather's eyes widen, at which Camden bursts out laughing.

"He's just kidding, you gits," she says. She rubs his chest and looks up into his eyes. "Right?"

"Of course, lovely Camden," he says. "I have never killed a Jehovah's Witness."

Jake clears his throat and gives Ortiz a look.

"I do not care what the official file said, Jake" Ortiz insists. "There is no way an East German Air Force officer was a Jehovah's Witness. No possible way."

"Always such a skeptic," Jake replies. No one else is quite sure what to say.

The next day Jake's engagement to Amy Sanders officially ends. She had been able to endure the long stretches of separation, even though she complained about it. She enjoyed telling her Sunday school class that her fiancé was out doing the Lord's work. She could have even overlooked the whole columnist/communist/priest controversy, since she still had no clue what he had actually said, and wasn't all that interested anyway. She had learned to tune out sermons when she was seven years old.

No, the deal breaker for her was the fact that several of her friends had seen Jake out with another woman. Her mother's hairdresser had actually been on the rooftop of the Dream Emporium the previous night and seen Jake with this woman. A much younger woman, apparently, and one that may or may not have been some kind of biker or punk musician. Embarrassing Amy in front of her friends is the one unforgivable sin.

Jake said nothing in his own defense, since all of her accusations were true. He was just happy it ended before they had the chance to do something really stupid, like actually get married.

It didn't even end face-to-face. He supposed he wasn't worth what she considered a long drive: he lived seven miles from her, which in Texas is the same as living next door. His phone rang, and the conversation went basically like this:

"Hello."

"Bastard," Amy said.

"Say again?"

"You heard me. I can't believe you're running around town with some floozy."

"She's actually a bookseller," he said.

"Do you have any clue how humiliating this is?"

"I've got a general idea."

"I'm not giving you the ring back," she said.

"It's *your* grandmother's ring."

"Bastard."

She slammed the phone down. All things being equal, he thought it went pretty well.

12

"A Story for Sal"

It is 11:00 a.m. and Max is at his table outside The Last Word. He has been here for over an hour, and in that time only two people have stopped, one to ask for directions to the Stockyards (*I think you go north from downtown until you see gang graffiti and smell cow dung*) and the other to say how cool his laptop is (*it's a typewriter, actually, not a laptop...oh, never mind*). Clouds are moving in from the west, and it looks like he will not even make ten bucks for one story today. Thank God Sal and Camden aren't making him pay for groceries yet.

He is about to pack up and call it a day when Sal comes outside to smoke. He offers Max one, and they walk a few steps down the sidewalk so the smoke will not blow across the front door as customers are entering, not that there have been any customers today. Having seen the ebb and flow of people at the store over the past weeks, Max wonders how booksellers manage to stay in business.

"It's dead around here today," Max says after Sal lights his cigarette.

"It'll pick up after lunch," Sal assures him. "That's the way Tuesdays seem to go around here, though I've never figured out why. I know that doesn't help you much, though, with your routine"

Sal knows that Max follows a fairly rigid schedule, at least when he hasn't been drinking heavily the night before. He will put in his time outside the store in the mornings, but by 1:00 p.m. he is either at a coffee shop working on his novel or upstairs typing up his handwritten drafts.

"At this rate I may have to change that routine or you will truly have taken me on to raise," Max says grimly. "I at least like to be able to pay for my own beer."

"I actually like it better when I don't have to pay for mine," Sal says with a laugh.

They finish their cigarettes at the same time and both flick the butts into the street. Max returns to his desk and Sal goes back inside. Less than five minutes later he is back.

"You know what I realized?" he asks. "In all the time you've been doing this flash fiction thing out here, I have never asked you to write a story for me."

"I actually thought about that," Max replies, "but I didn't want to mention it. I thought it might look pushy or, worse, like begging."

"Max, I'm the fan that asked you to come live with us. I made you sign all my copies of your books. How could you even consider letting me miss this opportunity?"

That makes Max smile. Over the time he's been here he and Sal have become friends, and he sometimes forgets that it was Sal's love of his books that rescued him from sleeping on park benches. He rolls a new clean sheet of paper into the old Royal.

"Very well, my friend," he says. "Give me a theme and I will write you the best on-the-spot story I can, free of charge of course."

"Oh, no," Sal says, pulling out his wallet. "It won't have the full effect if I don't pay."

He places a fifty-dollar bill on the table, sliding it under Max's coffee mug so it doesn't blow away. Max shakes his head.

"Too much," he protests. "I can't take it."

"You'll change your mind after I tell you what I want in the story," he says with a mischievous grin. "I want mine to be unique."

"Unique, huh?" Max says. "So you have given this some thought, even though you never asked me before."

"A little," Sal agrees. "First of all, I want something...how to put it...criminal. Doesn't have to be about the mob or anything, but that direction."

Max nods, marveling that of all the sidewalk stories people have asked him to write, both here and when he was in Brooklyn, crime is by far the most popular topic, with only ghost stories coming close. Maybe he should write horror detective novels.

"I also want it to be local, but not about the bookstore; that's too obvious. Maybe use that bar Jake's family owns, The Blarney Stone. You've been there with me."

Max nods again; not a bad setting, to be honest.

"I want Jake's old man, James Donovan, to be a character," he continues. "Jake won't mind because he'll never see this."

This is getting very specific, and Max starts to wonder if 50 bucks is enough. "Why him, exactly?" he asks.

"He's the only real criminal legend around here," Sal explains. "And I never got to meet him. They called him the Shamrock."

"Got it. Is that all?" He hopes that is all; the more specific the details the longer it will take to write.

"That would be good enough," Sal says. "But if you can work in two more things I'll add another $50."

"Wow," Max says. "I can't say no to that. What are they?"

"I want some kind of reference to Camden and Julia in it," he says. "And I want it in the first-person."

"You don't ask for much," Max says. "This is going to take a bit of time. Do you think I could get an Irish coffee to put me in the right frame of mind?"

"By all means."

Nearly an hour later, just as he's about to leave for lunch, Sal sees Max motioning to him through the front window. He walks outside and Max hands him three sheets of paper. It seems a little thin for $100, assuming he worked everything in, but it is flash fiction after all.

"See what you think," Max says, offering Sal his chair. He then bums a cigarette and a light and moves to a bench across the street so Sal can read without being tempted to ask questions.

Sal leans back in the chair, looks at the title and laughs. The sneaky bastard worked in a Camden reference before the story even starts.

Union Jack

I'm sitting at the bar minding my own damn business when a 300 pound leprechaun stumbles over his elf shoes and nearly knocks me off my stool. Green beer sloshes out of my mug and onto the floor. St. Patrick's Day in an Irish bar comes with hazards, and Lucky here is the least of them. I look at his green elf hat and glass eye with the shamrock for a pupil and remember arresting him about a year ago.

Even calling The Blarney Stone an Irish bar seems a stretch. The décor is more what you would find in a kitschy Italian restaurant, the walls covered with photographs of Italian celebrities ranging from Sinatra to the Pope. The only evidence of an Emerald Isle connection is a large Irish flag above the stage and a sign that reads: *"Dogs and Englishmen Not Allowed."*

Ethnicity aside, it's a typical college hangout with one notable exception: no dance floor. That's only noticeable because of the number of girls trying to dance beside the tables. Each time a girl's hips move more than they would when walking, a bouncer rushes over and stops them.

"Well good evening, my boy," a voice says coldly from the other side of the bar. *"Another beer?"*

I look over and see James Donovan: bar owner, father of my new girlfriend Julia, mobster.

"Hello, sir. Sure."

He leans down to grab a mug and catches a glimpse of the tattoo peeking beneath the edge of my sleeve.

"What the fuck is that?" he snarls.

I push the sleeve further up my bicep to reveal a Union Jack inside the outline of a heart.

"It's a tattoo."

"Don't be a wise-ass, boy," Donovan says. *"You see that sign over there?"* He points to the *"No Dogs or Englishmen"* sign.

"I saw it, but I'm a Texan. It's my mom who's English. From Manchester."

"Figures. And what about your dad? He a bloody Brit too?"

"German. And a Federal Prosecutor."

Donovan's face flushes crimson, but before he can speak someone is behind me, tapping me on the shoulder.

"Your table's ready, sir."

I turn to see a waitress, maybe 18 years old with dyed-green hair, holding a tray of drinks. She gives me a quick smile.

"Right this way. There's an empty table over here."

I slide off the stool, but Donovan stops me.

"Is that true about your dad?" he asks. I knew that would get him.

"No," I lie. "He's actually a mechanic, but after you disrespected my mom…"

Donovan smiles, then nods.

The waitress seats me at a small table near the stage and puts down a shot. She turns to leave but I put a hand on her arm.

"Why is there no dancing allowed?"

"Zoning ordinance," she says. "We're too close to the First Baptist Church."

Before I can ask what the hell this means there's a deafening crash a few tables away. Then shouting and fists flying and the smack of bones and muscle. A wild-eyed, solid man wades into the scrum, cracking guys' heads, knees, backs, shoulders with a sawed-off pool cue as he goes. It's Eddie Donovan, Julia's brother. I recognize him from the mug shot the Feds gave me.

One beefy guy punches a bystander in the face, who crumples in a heap. Eddie steps from his blind side, dislocates his knee with the cue, and cracks the guy on top of the head as he falls. His blood spurts across Eddie's face, but Eddie just keeps swinging his pool cue. His father sprints to his side faster than I expect for a man of his bulk.

"Hey, you little shit," he says, glaring down at the guy, "stop bleeding on my floor." His voice is cold, flat, devoid of emotion.

"I've got him, Pop," Eddie says, grabbing the man by the collar.

Old man Donovan claps a meaty hand on his son's shoulder.

"We pay people for that kind of scut work, son," he says, and steers Eddie back to the bar. Both men grin at me, shove through the gawking crowd and past my table; Eddie slaps the bloody pool cue into his open palm.

The show now over, I throw back the shot of whiskey the waitress left.

Suddenly the crazy-eyed brother is back, sitting at my table, still slapping the pool cue into his palm. His smile has vanished, his mouth now a tight slit, and blood still drips from his face; for a second I think I'll have to shoot him, which will totally fuck my cover. Before I can reach for the gun in my boot Julia appears behind her brother. She grabs one of his ears and jerks down hard, yanking him out of the chair and onto his knees.

"Jesus!" he screams. "Let me go, you crazy bitch!"

"I told you not to pull any of your crazy macho shit," she screams back. She looks over at her father, who is grinning broadly. "I told both of you."

She throws a vicious knee into her brother's spine and he pitches face-first onto the floor.

"Let's go," she says. "There's an English pub down the street with a more agreeable clientele."

We walk past her father behind the bar.

"Enjoy your evening lad," he says. "My daughter won't always be around to protect you."

As we stride across the parking lot I grab her hand; it feels hot. I glance at her face; she is flushed and beaming. At that moment I realize my new angel could be the most dangerous Donovan of all. Maybe I'll use my handcuffs on her later.

Max returns just as Sal is finishing the last paragraph. He looks up, laughing uncontrollably, and then pulls out his wallet. He slides two twenties and a ten under the coffee mug.

"You made me a cop," he says, still laughing.

"I made the protagonist a cop," Max corrects him. "A writer never uses real people in his stories; that would make him a biographer." He barely gets this out before he starts laughing too.

Sal looks again at the bottom of the last page. The handwritten inscription above Max's signature reads: *For Sal, who showed me you really can start over.*

"Perfect," he says as he stands up from the table. "Let's grab some lunch."

13

"Discount Books"

"There's no money to be made selling used books, Sal," Jacob says after Sal mentions that used books are a market the store has yet to tap. "Discount Books will undersell us anyway, which is why your uncle got rid of the small used section we had years ago."

"I have told you never to mention that place in my presence," Sal says. "It was bad enough having one of them in Trenton. Then I move down here and find one on every freaking corner."

Discount Books had been founded in the early 1970s by two Dallas men escaping the corporate rat race. They opened their first store in an abandoned dry cleaner's on Royal Lane with two thousand books from their personal libraries, and had built the business over the decades into the Wal-Mart of bookstores. They now had over 100 locations in 20 states. They bought and sold used books, magazines, DVDs, CDs, and vinyl records.

It wasn't their success that Sal and Jacob resented, exactly; a few chain stores had even been good for the book business over the years. It was the rather the way Discount Books had, in every city where they had opened a store, run every used bookstore already operating there out of business. And they did it the old-fashioned way: when they first opened a store they would offer abnormally high prices for the books they bought from customers. They could do this because they were large enough to absorb losses at one or two stores in the chain for the first year or so. They could also bring in overstock from other stores, so their shelves were always full.

After a period of time, the small independent used bookstores couldn't replenish their stock because they couldn't compete with the high prices that Discount Books was paying customers for their books. Their shelves became bare, and fewer and fewer people shopped there. Ultimately, they all closed. And once they were gone, Half Price would suddenly stop paying those great prices and pay less than you'd get at a garage sale. But now they were the only game in town. They were a literary Wal-Mart.

They had upped the ante with two recent developments. After Borders and Barnes & Noble put many of the independent bookstores that sold new books out of business, Discount Books saw a void they could fill: they began selling new bestsellers at a discounted price that even Barnes & Noble couldn't match, moving for the first time outside of the used book market. Second, and far less forgivable, was an alliance with the bane of indie bookstores everywhere: Blue Nile. They had set up a partnership with the online giant to sell their books online as well as in stores, joining with the Great Satan to further destroy the bookselling ecosystem that first gave the company life.

"There is money to be made," Sal says, "otherwise we wouldn't let you buy the used books you buy." He knows that calling the stock of Jacob's Rare and Collectible Room "used" will hit a nerve.

"The books I buy are not 'used,' as you so crassly call them. They are valuable rare editions, all first printings, many with fine bindings...you're just winding me up, aren't you?"

"Yep," Sal says with a laugh. "Works every time. Seriously though, why can't we add used books to our inventory?"

"Look," Jacob says, "I know you don't like the way they seem to gobble up every book in town like some Japanese fishing trawler. I don't like it either, but it's the reality of things today. They can operate on a huge scale because of all the stores they have."

"Scale has nothing to do with it," Sal counters. "Ok, maybe a little, but mainly what they do is blow into town, offer more for people's books than any of the established used bookstores can afford, and then once the competition is eliminated they start offering pennies on the dollar because there's nowhere else for people to sell their books."

"That's called business," Camden says, walking up for the tail-end of his rant, but having heard it many times before.

"It's crap," Sal says.

"Perhaps," Jacob says, "but you really don't want to get into that side of the book business, trust me. People bring in the most worthless stuff and expect a fortune for it. You would spend half your day looking at beat up copies of diet books, celebrity biographies, World Book encyclopedias, and Reader's Digest Condensed Books."

Jake shudders at his last four words, as Jacob knew he would. He despises the RDCBs.

"There has to be a way," he persists, "for us to get the word out that we will pay more than Discount Books for good copies of certain kinds of books. I mean, look at you Jacob. People bring you their collectible stuff."

"Because they know we offer a fair price for excellent copies," he says. "That's going to be harder to convey to people on common books, even if you confine the used stock to fiction. Some people see no difference between Faulkner and Tom Clancy, though clearly there is a huge difference."

"Right," Camden says. "Clancy sells ten times as many books." She stares at them blankly for a long moment, and then bursts out laughing. "I'm kidding, you twits. I am not against the idea, Sal, but how does it help the store?" To her astonishment, he actually has an answer ready.

"One way would be required reading lists," he says. "High school kids' parents don't want to pay for all new books if they can avoid it, but also can rarely find everything they need at a place like Discount Books. Here they can get everything in one stop, and save a little by picking up whatever used copies we do have."

"Interesting idea," she mutters.

"And while you may never have encountered this situation, being a soulless accountant, there are also readers out there who would love to own a houseful of books but can't afford new-book prices. We can meet a need there as well."

"Not as compelling an argument, but ok," she says. "Anything else?"

"As a matter of fact, yes. We will start small, then expand, then open a store in every town Discount Books has one, and ultimately we will crush those thieving bastards into dust."

"Quite. A fine plan all the way round," Camden says. "Such a shame we don't have any space left for a used books section." Sal gazes around the packed store and his shoulders slump.

"You could always use the basement," Jacob says casually as he flips through a collection of Pasternak's poems. Sal and Camden turn and stare at him as if he is speaking a foreign language.

"Jacob," Camden says in her most soothing voice, "we don't have a basement."

"Early onset senility," Sal whispers.

"Of course you do," Jacob says, closing the book. "You've been in this building more than a year…you *live* in this building, for crying out loud…and didn't know there was a basement? How is that possible?"

It is obvious now that he is neither joking nor senile. Maybe they actually do have a basement. Camden looks at Sal, who shrugs.

"I guess it's possible," he says. "I've never looked in the attic, but I know there is one. So where is this mythical basement, Mr. Weinberg? Wait, before you give me a smart-ass answer, let me rephrase that: where is the entrance to this mythical basement?"

Jacob suddenly looks less certain, and far less cocky.

"Well," he says hesitantly. "It's been a long time, more than 20 years. But I know there was an entrance somewhere."

"*Somewhere?*" Camden repeats. "Are you telling us you know we have a basement but don't know how to get to it?"

"Like I said, it's been more than 20 years since I saw it. I don't even know what made me think of it just now…something from one of the Pasternak poems, I suppose. Franklin didn't like it, so he kept it closed off and never used it."

"Why didn't my uncle like it?" Sal asks.

"He said it felt like a tomb," Jacob replies. "If I remember correctly it's just one big room, with concrete walls and floor and a couple bare light bulbs."

"At least it has electricity and isn't just a dirt floored storm cellar," Sal muses. "It just might work, assuming we can find this hidden entrance to the underworld. Camden, have Ramon start looking for that door."

"Why can't you look for it?" she asks. "This is your idea after all."

"I would, but Jacob and I have to leave for a few hours."

"Where are we going?" Jacob asks, instantly suspicious.

"We are going to do some reconnaissance on our used-book competition," he says. "Cam, if you need us, we'll be at the Discount Books on Forest Park Blvd."

Sal has never been inside the Discount Books on Forest Park, even though it is only a few miles from the store, but he has a strong feeling of déjà vu as soon as they walk inside. It takes him a second to realize that the store is set up exactly like the one back in Trenton (which he had been in a few times). Not a lot like, *exactly* like.

Apparently those two Dallas entrepreneurs, who still owned the company, had the concept of chain store down to an art: plain, unvarnished wooden bookcases in long rows, buying counter to the left as you walk in, checkout counter right at the front, and along both side walls little alcoves formed from the U-shaped placement of the bookcases, each with a different subject. There were art books, science books, gardening, sports, biographies, music, history, politics, and a number of other topics that they had wisely decided to avoid at The Last Word. The long rows in the middle contained all of the fiction genres; this was where Sal would start. He turns to say something to Jacob, but he has already made a beeline for their collectible section.

Sal wanders down the fiction aisles, noticing that while they are full, much of the space is taken up by a handful of best-selling authors. This makes sense, of course; best-sellers are exactly that for a reason. But there is something depressing in the fact that there are roughly nine shelves of nothing but Janet Evanovich books, 11 shelves of Stephen King, and 21 (*twenty-one!*) shelves containing only the prolific James Patterson. By contrast, Somerset Maugham rates exactly four books (not shelves), Gabriel Garcia Marquez has eight books, and Virginia Woolf only two.

He walks over to where Jacob is examining a shelf marked "Signed and First Editions."

"We're not in competition with these guys," Sal whispers to him. "We're not even selling the same books. Heather would have a heart attack if she saw what they pass off as literature."

"It's much worse than that," Jacob says gravely. He hands a book to Sal, who looks at the cover then flips it open, first to the front flyleaf where the price is written in pencil, then the title page and finally to the copyright page.

His eyes widen. He looks around for an employee, finally flagging down a girl of about 18 who could be Heather's little sister.

"Who does the pricing for the collectible books?" Sal asks.

"Whoever happens to be working when the book comes in," she says. "Why?"

He shows her the book he's holding. "You have this book marked as a signed first edition, and priced at $95.00," he says.

"Is there something wrong with the book?"

"Well," Jacob says, stepping up beside Sal. "For one thing, while it technically is a first *edition,* it is a fourth printing. See how the number line at the bottom of the page starts with a 4? Anything other than a first printing is virtually worthless to collectors. Also, this particular author is notorious for signing every book he can get his hands on; there are probably more signed copies in circulation than unsigned ones."

"Which means what exactly?" the girl asks, clearly losing interest.

"Which means," Sal says, "your $95.00 book is actually worth about ten bucks."

"Buyer beware, I guess," she says. "I'm more of a music expert myself. So do you want that book? I could probably get the manager to knock the price down to $50 or something."

"But it's not worth even half that," Sal says, exasperated with this girl.

"So you say. Remember, we're the experts." With this she turns and walks away.

Sal looks at Jacob, shrugs, and puts the book back on the shelf. Some poor idiot will come in one day and pay an insane price for a worthless book. Unfortunately it happened all the time, especially to people who bought "rare" books online.

"Let's get out of here Sal," Jacob says. "This place depresses me."

"Give me one more minute," Sal says. "I want to check something."

"Have you not seen enough?"

"I have, including something very interesting."

"What's that?" Jacob asks.

"Look over at the kid at the checkout counter," Sal says. "He's keying in the prices of all the books that woman's buying."

"So?"

"All of the books in this store have bright yellow stickers with the price and a barcode at the top. Why is he manually entering the price into the register if there's a barcode?"

"I don't know, I don't care, and I don't know why you care."

"I'm intrigued," Sal says. "And I have the germ of an idea, but I need to confirm something first."

He walks over to the counter, and after the woman has left with her books he steps up to the clerk, a hipster in his mid-20s with a "Darth Vader is my Father" T-shirt.

"Can I help you, sir?" he asks.

"Yeah," Sal asks. "I'm looking for a book and was wondering if you have it in stock. It's called *Sad Movies*, by Mark Lindquist." Sal purposely chose this book not just because he likes it, but because it is nearly impossible to find anywhere.

"Let me get someone to check the shelf for you," the young man says.

"I checked the shelf," Sal says. "I thought maybe you had it in the back, or even at one of your other stores if not."

"Sorry, sir," the clerk says, shaking his head. "We're not fully computerized yet, so there's no way to know what we have in the back or at any of our other stores. The goal is to have the system up and working in the next year or so, but that's a big change for us."

"But you have barcodes on your price stickers," Sal says.

The guy looks around, then leans across the counter and whispers to Sal.

"The barcodes are just for show," he says conspiratorially. "The higher-ups think they make us look more professional and deter theft at the same time. See the detectors at the front door? Those aren't plugged into anything." He opens a drawer and shows Sal stacks of prices stickers, each stack denoting a different price. "If you look closely at the barcodes you'll see that they're actually all the same."

"That's nuts," Sal says.

"Hard to keep up technologically when you're growing as fast as this company is. We're opening four more stores next month alone."

"Well, thanks anyway. I guess I'll just have to keep looking."

"Have you tried The Last Word downtown?" the guy asks. "I hear they have a lot of good stuff. Plus, the owner was supposedly a hit man for the Colombian drug cartels."

"Is that so?" Sal asks with a laugh, and he and Jacob leave the abomination that is Discount Books.

14

"The Great Price Tag Caper"

Sal slips down the short alley off 8th Street just past Houston. He moves quickly down a flight of concrete steps that lead to what at first glance appears to be the basement of the Robber Baron's Restaurant directly above. In reality it is a completely separate establishment, by night the raucous Bop Jazz Lounge and by day the quietest place to drink in town. Once inside his eyes struggle to adjust to the dim lighting, but after a moment he sees Jake and Ortiz seated at a booth in the far corner.

There had been a time when Sal spent the better part of his day in places like this, but since taking over the bookstore he only drank during the day occasionally. His definition of occasionally differed somewhat from Camden's, but she had been an accountant after all. He is confident, however, that none of the ladies at the store will even think to look for them here, if they even know the place exists. He takes a seat at the table, noticing that Ortiz and Jake are already halfway through a pitcher of beer.

"I didn't think preachers were allowed to drink in the middle of the day," he tells Jake with a smile.

"Technically we're not allowed to drink at all," Jake says as he fills Sal's mug. "I've never been too good at following rules."

"Where are the others?" Ortiz asks. "We can't do this with three people."

"We decided it was best to leave the store at different times," Sal says. "Less likely to arouse suspicion."

"Let me go on record that I have not yet agreed to be a part of this foolishness," Jake says. "And that's what it looks like to me; a foolish prank that could get you thrown in jail if you get caught."

"Get caught?" Sal repeats in mock horror. "Us? Never."

"It is a fact, Jake," Ortiz agrees. "We have never been caught, either one of us."

"That's been true until now," Jake says. "But bookman here is out of practice, and you're not getting any younger."

"This particular job requires no skill," Ortiz replies. "I am not even convinced that it is illegal. Any reputable judge would simply chuckle and send me on my way, perhaps with a nice mojito and some tapas."

"Of course," Jake laughs. "Judges always give criminals alcohol and appetizers after the trial. How silly of me."

They continue this banter until Jacob and Max arrive. Sal is still not thrilled about involving them but both insisted, Max because he thought it would be fun, and Jacob because he is still incensed over what he saw in Discount Books' signed and first edition section. Max pours himself a beer; Jacob asks for iced tea. Sal leans in close so he will not be overheard, even though the only other people in the bar are the waitress and the bartender.

"I went back yesterday and again last night to check everything out," he says. "If it wasn't for the sheer volume I could do the whole thing myself, but that's not practical. I appreciate all of you agreeing to join me, and I assume you are aware of the risks, legally speaking."

"The only risk I can see," Max says, "is getting charged with trespassing."

"Incorrect, my literary friend," Ortiz says. "A particularly zealous prosecutor could choose from a range of offenses: trespassing, yes, but also breaking and entering, vandalism, intent to defraud, criminal mischief. All petty crimes to be sure, but taken together they could be quite serious."

"What about the mojitos and tapas?" Jake asks.

"I was talking only about myself then," Ortiz replies. "I have a way with judges, especially lady judges."

"We will not get caught," Sal assures them. "I never get caught. But if by some act of God it did happen, the only ones here with any kind of prior records are me and Ortiz. And other than a youthful indiscretion by Luis that was expunged by exemplary military service, neither of us have ever been convicted."

"What about the alarm system?" Jake asks. "And the surveillance cameras? And the security guard?"

Max and Jacob turn to Sal expectantly; these are things they have not considered. Ortiz stifles a yawn.

"For a guy who snuck in and out of hostile countries for a living you sure do worry a lot," Sal says to Jake. "But they are fair questions. The security guard, one guy for the whole strip mall, is a couple years older than Moses and sleeps most of the night after he does his first rounds of the night. There are no surveillance cameras – I guess that's another technology their management is working on – and the alarm system is a joke."

"It worries me that you're making this whole thing sound so simple," Jake says.

"It is simple, just really time consuming. You don't have to come if you're that worried."

Jake's eyes flash angrily for a moment, and Ortiz places a huge hand on his shoulder. In that instant Sal sees the man whose job it was to kill people from long distances; he makes a mental note to tread lightly around him tonight. In an effort to release the tension building up, he rolls out a diagram he has made of the store, complete with times noted on the right margin.

"We get in, do what we have to do, and we get out," he says. "With five of us it should take a couple hours max. So is everyone in?"

All of the men at the table nod. Jacob seems almost giddy, Max determined, Jake wary, and Ortiz bored. Sal is simply calm, as he always is before a job, though this is like no job he's ever pulled before.

""Good," he says. "We go at midnight."

By the following afternoon news has reached the store of the riot at Discount Books. Ramon heard about it from a friend who works at a shoe store in the same strip mall, and he is telling everyone in The Last Word the story.

"Jaime said the morning started out normal," Ramon says, "but by noon the parking lot was packed and there was a line to get into the bookstore. He thought maybe they were having one of those big sales they do a couple times a year, but those are normally advertised weeks ahead of time.

"He could see people coming out of the store pushing cartloads of books, like entire shopping carts *full,* so he walked over to check it out. He asked one of the customers coming out what was going on, and they told him that almost every book in the store was on sale for 99 cents."

"99 cents?" Camden repeats, stunned. "How is that possible? Even the hardcovers?"

"Yeah," Ramon says. "That got Jaime's attention for sure, because he loves science fiction, but can't afford it in hardcover; he buys paperbacks from us. So he pushed his way into the store to try and pick up some Heinlein and Asimov."

"Sal," Camden says, "if they can sell everything at 99 cents we are in huge trouble."

"Fear not, cousin," Sal says reassuringly. "Our stock is very different from theirs, and I bet that sale won't last forever. Right, Jacob?"

""I imagine it will be a one-day phenomenon," Jacob replies.

"Not even that long," Ramon says. "Jaime had just paid for an armload of books when the manager showed up; apparently he had been at a meeting at the main store in Dallas."

"The Flagship," Sal says derisively.

"No one had bothered to call to tell him what was happening, and he went nuts. Started screaming at the employees that they were idiots, asking how the hell all the prices got changed, threatening to fire everyone. Then he announced that the store was closed and everyone had to leave."

"Which is when the riot broke out," Julia says.

"Yep," Ramon says. "Jaime said he feared for his life the way the crowd reacted, and this is a kid who's been in the East Side Homeboys since he was twelve years old. He said no banger with a gun is as scary as an old woman with an armload of 99 cent Danielle Steel hardbacks being told the sale is off."

"What did they all do?" Julia asks excitedly. "Refuse to leave?"

"Jaime was just trying to get out at this point," Ramon says. "He said some refused to leave, some threw their books down and screamed obscenities at the manager, and then it got ugly."

"Sounds like it was already pretty ugly," Sal says, trying to suppress a smile.

"Jaime was at the door when the manager threatened to have everyone arrested. That's when the old ladies started pelting him with romance paperbacks. He pushed his way to the back and locked himself in the storeroom. Jaime said the cops showed up about 15 minutes later, but by then the store had been stripped bare."

"How in the world can that have happened?" Camden wonders aloud. "Was it a computer glitch?"

"No," Ramon says. "Jaime said the price stickers on the books all said 99 cents. And they were the stickers the store normally uses."

"Besides," Sal says, "their computer system doesn't work."

The words are out of his mouth before he realizes he's said them, and he knows immediately that he has made a huge mistake. Everyone turns and stares at him except Jacob; he moves quickly and quietly to his rare book room and closes the door.

"How do you know their computer system doesn't work?" Julia asks. She is not smiling.

"One of their clerks told me when Jacob and I were in there the other day."

"And where were you last night?" she asks.

"You cannot possibly believe that I broke into Discount Books and managed to put new stickers on all their books by myself," he replies, carefully avoiding answering her question.

At that moment Max comes downstairs from the apartment. He looks like he's still half-asleep.

"I'm not as young as I used to be," he says, walking past them toward the door. "After all that work last night I need a double espresso."

The bell about the door chimes as he leaves. Camden and Julia watch him go, then turn back to Sal.

"No," Julia says, "you couldn't do it alone. But if you had help…"

"I am shocked that you would accuse me of such a juvenile prank," Sal protests. "I am a highly respected bookseller and was, allegedly, a very competent thief. A job like that would be beneath my dignity." They continue to stare at him. "But if by chance I ever was to engage in such tomfoolery, it would not violate my promise to you, Julia, to never rob anyone again, since clearly nothing was taken from the store."

Julia tries to hold her stern expression, but now Camden is giggling. After a few seconds Julia can't help herself; she starts laughing too. Ramon seems puzzled by the entire exchange, but he has more news that he needs to share with Sal.

"I found the basement, Mr. Sal," he says. "The door was hidden by the bookcase where we keep the children's chapter books. I measured to see how many bookcases we can fit down there, and I think I can hang some fluorescent lights without having to call an electrician."

"Excellent job, my young friend," Sal says happily. "Let's order some bookcases and start loading up on used books. I think our friends at Discount have a public relations problem that we can exploit if we move quickly enough."

Julia moves close to Sal and kisses him on the cheek.

"So was it like old times?" she asks.

"Not even close."

15

"The Writing Life"

Max does not much like talking to groups, particularly groups who wanted to know the "secret" to writing. He does, however, like to eat three meals a day and sleep under a roof whenever possible. On a stormy Wednesday evening these conflicting attitudes are colliding as a result of his new role as Writer in Residence at The Last Word. A glance outside at the driving rain and the smell of the food piled on a side table makes the choice a simple one.

Camden had wanted him to stand at a podium to address the crowd of budding authors that is still gathering in the open space near the children's section, while Julia had thought an interview-style arrangement, with one of the staff asking pre-arranged questions, might be more comfortable for him. In the end it is Sal who has the idea that most fits Max's personality: they set up the table, chair, and manual typewriter he had been using outside at the front of the space, and he sat there, his battered old Royal providing a comforting psychological shield between him and the crowd.

Sal does him the added favor of providing him with a large mug that is half black coffee and half bourbon. Max takes a satisfying sip and looks out over the assembled crowd; as he had expected, there are probably twice as many women as men. In his early years this would have meant literary groupies, but today it simply reflects the reality that more women are writing than men. The sad corresponding reality is that the men still have a much better chance of getting published. Self-publishing was leveling the field somewhat, but progress was slow.

This fact angers Max. He had patterned himself after Hemingway, but if Papa were here he would be the first to admit that he never wrote a sentence as beautiful as the ones Virginia Woolf considered unfit to publish. Jane Austen, the Bronte sisters, Ursula K. Le Guin, and Isabel Allende, to name only a few, were amazing writers who too often were described as amazing *female* writers. His new favorite, Zadie Smith, was so much better than that hack Jonathan Franzen (he had met both of them in Brooklyn) that it was a crime that Franzen outsold her ten to one.

Heather walks to the front and motions for quiet. Sal and Camden own the place, but the literature section is her kingdom; by extension Max, and this gathering, fall under her purview. She has upgraded her wardrobe for the occasion: she wears black jeans instead of blue, has shined her Doc Martens, and has even thrown a tasteful black blazer over her "Joan Jett is My Mom" T-shirt.

"I want to thank all of you for coming to the first writer's workshop here at The Last Word," she says, her voice projecting perfectly through the meeting space. "We are thrilled to have Max Luther with us tonight. Mr. Luther is the author of the critically acclaimed novels *Liquid Time* and *Midnight in Trafalgar Square*, to name just a few. He recently became Writer in Residence here at the store, and has graciously agreed to share his wealth of knowledge about writing and publishing with us tonight. So let's begin."

She turns to Max, gives a half-bow, and retreats to the side of the room where Sal and Camden are seated. For a moment people seem unsure if they are supposed to applaud, then decide almost as one that they should, and the slight delay is awkward, though Max is unfazed as he drinks deeply from his mug.

"Let me start by saying that contrary to the Wikipedia entry, I am not actually dead," Max says. This elicits sustained laughter from the group, which is always a good way to start.

"I corrected that this morning," Heather says. "Now you are just gravely ill."

More laughter. Time for Max to bring the mood back down.

"My advice to all of you," Max says gravely, "is to leave now. Take up scrapbooking or the bassoon or rabbit breeding. Become a rodeo clown or a blacksmith or an encyclopedia salesman. All of these are preferable to pursuing a life as a writer."

The laughter turns uncomfortable and then stops completely.

"If you're in this for the money," he continues, "you will probably make more over your lifetime by collecting aluminum cans for recycle. But then if you're only in it for the money, you'll never write anything worth a damn anyway."

A young girl, no more than 15 or 16 years old, holds up her hand. Max nods at her.

"Aren't you supposed to be encouraging us to be writers?" she asks. "Isn't that the point?"

"I am supposed to tell you the truth, young lady," he replies. "And the truth is that this is perhaps the hardest, most frustrating, least financially rewarding career path you can take. I need to make that clear up front. Unless, of course, you are only writing as a hobby and have no intention of anyone ever reading your work." He pauses and looks around the room. "Anyone here just writing as a hobby?"

A man in his twenties seated in the back row raises his hand. He's dressed in khakis and a golf shirt and is grinning idiotically. Max nods approvingly.

"An honest answer," Max says. "Now get out. I'm not here to talk about keeping diaries; you should have learned that in junior high."

The man continues grinning, but no one else is smiling. Max does not say another word. The silence stretches to a minute, then several minutes. Finally the man rises from his chair, mutters "asshole," and leaves the store.

"Right," Max says once he is gone. "Now at least I know I'm talking to people who are serious. Misguided and likely doomed to alcoholism, poverty and failure, but serious."

The laughter returns, and Max lifts his cup to Sal: he needs a refill. When Sal moves forward to take the cup another woman, this one in her mid forties with an intense expression, speaks up.

"Is it really that hard?" she asks. "After all, you're a successful writer, so it can be done, right?"

Max had intended to move on from the warning phase of his talk, but that would have to wait a little longer.

"There is some debate over the exact numbers," he says, "but this is a fact: there are more people playing in the National Football League, roughly 1500, than there are writers who make a full-time living solely from their writing. The average income for a writer is around $10,000 a year, and that's with people like Stephen King and James Patterson pulling the average up with their astronomical earnings."

"But you –" the woman persists.

"I have had three very successful novels, by both critical and commercial standards, and several more that were good to adequate. Yet I currently call home a couch in an apartment above a bookstore, and I own neither the bookstore, nor the apartment nor the couch. Even in really good times I usually had a second job. My favorite was teaching early 20th century literature at Grover Washington High School in the Bronx."

This time a young man in a "Meat is Murder" T-shirt speaks up.

"Grover Washington the saxophone player?" he asks." He has a school named after him?"

Max stares blankly at him for a split second.

"Ah, make that Grover Cleveland High School," he says, his voice less gruff than it has been all evening. "I forgot to mention dementia as one of the results of being a writer."

This is enough to lighten the mood again, and Heather seizes the opportunity to change the direction of the discussion.

"Tell them about meeting Hemingway!" she shouts.

The room is instantly silent, all eyes expectantly on Max. Even the ones who don't like Hemingway know that he is in the Pantheon of authors.

"I did meet Hemingway," he says, smiling at the memory. "I was only eight or nine years old and we were in Key West on vacation. I had already read *The Old Man and the Sea* and *A Farewell to Arms* even at that young age, and when I saw him walking down the street one morning I was awestruck. He looked exactly like all of the caricatures of him now do, like all those guys who enter the lookalike contest in Key West every year: white beard, overweight, sailor's cap, magnificent. You have to understand, he was a celebrity then, at a time when you actually had to have accomplished something to be a celebrity, but to me it was like seeing God."

"And you talked to him?" asks a girl born at least 20 years after Papa died.

"I did," Max says. "I asked him for his autograph - again, this was before people charged for autographs - and handed him a paperback copy of some detective novel I had in my back pocket, one of those with the lurid covers you don't see any more. He asked me my name, and I told him. I also blurted out that I wanted to be a writer just like him."

Several people in the crowd nodded, and the irony of the fact that he was now talking to aspiring writers was not lost on Max.

"He wrote a short description, patted me on the head, and went on his way."

"What did he write?" Heather asks excitedly. She knew about the meeting, but Max had not mentioned the inscription.

"He wrote: *To Max, Keep on writing, but fishing is a more enviable vocation. Ernest Hemingway.* I wonder sometimes if he wasn't right."

"Do you still have the book?" a girl in a plaid jumper asks. "I bet it's worth a lot of money now if you do."

Max nods. "I still have it," he says, "and it probably is worth a tidy sum, maybe even enough for me to buy my own couch. But I have never had it appraised, and will never sell it. The value of some things can't be measured in financial terms, things like love, friendship, a Hemingway inscription to a young boy, and a well-written story."

"You don't sound so cynical now," observes the Meat is Murder kid.

"Oh, I'm as cynical as ever," Max assures him. "I just understand that, for me at least, there is no other option except to write, so I place a high value on the written word. That may end up being true for some of you as well. For most, in all honesty, it won't. Life will get in the way, other things will take precedence, and the dream will fade. If the dream doesn't fade, the best advice I can offer is what Hemingway offered me: keep on writing."

"What do you think about self-publishing?" a man close to Max's age asks. "Is it a valid option?"

Max rubs his chin and takes another drink of bourbon-laced coffee. Whether because of the liquor or the memory of meeting Papa he is not sure, but he is warming up to these eager, would-be authors.

"Years ago," he says, wiping coffee from his upper lip, "when the only way to self-publish was by paying a vanity press thousands of dollars to print a few hundred copies that would never sell, I would have said no, it's not valid. Today, with print-on-demand so affordable and the technology improving so rapidly, not to mention the potential of e-books, I would say go for it." He pauses and then adds, "Of course, I have been fired by four publishers and at least that many blood-sucking agents, so my opinion is somewhat biased."

There is a sudden rush of sound, everyone talking over each other trying to ask questions. This is clearly a hot topic with them. Heather takes a step forward and motions for quiet.

"One at a time please," she says. "Yes, ma'am?" She points to a petite woman who in addition to being an aspiring author has also purchased nearly every cozy mystery the store has in stock. The room settles down and the woman stands to ask her question.

"Why do you call agents blood-suckers?" she asks. "Aren't they the only way to get your book in front of publishers?"

"Almost without exception," Max answers bitterly, "which is one of many reasons they are blood-suckers. They get 15% of your earnings, *for life*, mainly for simply getting your manuscript through the front door of the publishing house. They are nothing more than the second readers for the publishers, a way of weeding through piles of manuscripts so the publishers don't have to."

"Second readers?" the petite lady repeats. "Who are the first readers?"

"The poorly paid and often barely literate interns the agents employ to wade through *their* slush pile. Their mission is to fly through manuscripts as fast as possible, rejecting 99% of them for everything from poor writing – there is a lot of that – to bad formatting to simple laziness."

"But don't the agents help in other ways?" Meat is Murder guy asks. "Like with advice on the book or contracts or something?"

"Nope," Max says flatly. "The editor gives advices on the novel, which is great if your editor is worth anything and not just a failed writer himself. Editing is a skill just like writing, and a good editor is crucial. For example, both Hemingway and Fitzgerald had Max Perkins as their editor. He was a master of his craft, and their books are immeasurably better because of the work he did."

"Contracts," he continues, "are handled by lawyers, a different breed of parasite that at least provides a necessary service for their pound of flesh. Agents do no real work, take an unreasonable percentage of your earnings, and can drop you the minute your sales lag."

"What kind of writing schedule do you follow?" asks the 15-year-old girl, clearly ready to move on from the unseemly business aspects to the more important process of actually writing.

Max has answered this as many different ways as times he has been asked the question, because he has never stuck to any particular method or schedule for any length of time.

"Right now I try to finish five handwritten pages a day," he says. He usually comes nowhere near that number, but they don't need to know that. "My best writing time is between 8:00 and 11:00 in the morning, if I'm awake and sober." The laughter is scattered, most unsure if he is joking. "You have to find your own most productive time, which may be morning, may be evening, or may even be the time in the middle of the afternoon when the kids are down for a nap. Whenever it may be, guard that time fiercely, because it is the most precious thing you have as a writer."

"You do your first draft by hand?" asks a burly man with a beard that reaches the middle of his chest. He wears a camo jacket and a shirt that says "America: Love It Or Else." "I had heard you still used a manual typewriter."

"I write the rough drafts on a legal pad," Max explains. "When I do the first revisions I type it up on the typewriter. By the time I move to the computer, a sadly necessary evil, what results from that revision is usually the final product, or close to it."

"But why not just use the computer to start with?" the burly Republican asks. "Seems like a lot of unnecessary work, from pen to typewriter to computer."

Max stares at him, wondering if he writes spy novels or techno-thrillers. More likely he writes steamy romance under a female pen name.

"It is a lot of work," Max agrees. "But using three different mediums forces me to look at the material three different perspectives. I write really fast longhand, which keeps me from editing myself as I go. I type slowly on the old typewriter, which helps me think about better ways to say what I wrote the first time. The computer is for polishing it up."

"Are you working on a new book?" an older lady with long silver hair asks.

"Always," Max replies. "You should always be working on the next book. The hardest thing for me has always been not continuing to rewrite the one that was just published. You have to send it out into the world, like a kid who's graduated from high school, and let it stand or fall on its own."

It is approaching closing time, and no one seems to have any more questions, so Heather steps to the front again.

"As a thank you for your attendance tonight we have a copy of *Liquid Time* for each of you, which Max will be glad to autograph. He will also sign any of his other books you have either brought with you or would like to purchase from our stock."

A small line forms at Max's table, while the rest of the group is shepherded to the fiction section of the store by Heather; a small display of Max's books is set up at the end of an aisle. Sal makes a quick count of the number of books that pass across the counter.

"Even giving away the copies of *Liquid Time* we're going to make a profit on the night," he says triumphantly to Camden.

She starts to point out that Max has cost far more than this in groceries alone, but seeing how happy Sal is she simply nods in agreement. It actually has been a pretty good plan after all.

16

"The Haunted House"

The line of cars stretches to infinity and beyond, or so it seems to Sal. *Of all the stupid ideas...*

"I can't believe I let you talk me into going to a 'haunted house' on Halloween night," he says.

"It will be fun," Julia assures him.

"I could be handing out candy to little kids, or stealing candy from little kids, or scaring the hell out of little kids." He cranes his neck in an attempt to see an end to the traffic, to no avail. "I'm turning around. It will be Thanksgiving before we get there."

"I have endured two months of Jets games for you, Terranova," she says sharply. "You *will* do this haunted house thing with me."

He can't argue with that, and endured is the right word; the Jets have been awful. He's not even sure she likes football.

"You know, you've never said who your favorite team is. I assume it's the Cowboys since you're from here. That would also explain why you've never said."

Not even the hint of a smile. He rolls down the window and is rewarded with a blast of chilly air. As if the car wasn't already cold enough.

"Don't try to change the subject," she says. "And it's not the Cowboys, it's the Raiders. Don't ask."

"The Raiders?" he repeats. "How is that possible?"

"I said don't ask."

"Come on, tell me," he prods. "Tell me and I'll tell where I really was the night of the Ithaca heist."

She cannot hold her stern tone at this.

"I know where you were," she says with a laugh. "And you know where you were. What you can never remember is where the alibi says you were."

"It's a deal then. Tell me."

"Fine," she says with a short sigh. "My grandparents on my mom's side are huge Cowboys fans, and on my dad's side they're huge Steelers fans."

"Oh, that's not good," he says in mock horror.

"You joke," she says, poking him in the ribs, "but try growing up with that. In any case, when my parents got serious after meeting at Stanford, they became Raiders fans in an attempt at détente. You should ask my mom about the story of their wedding; that's when they came out, so

174

to speak. My grandparents weren't happy, but they accepted it."

"I sense a 'but' coming."

"Yeah. Apparently it was okay for my parents, but raising the grandchildren to be Raiders fans as well was a bridge too far. We haven't seen them, either side, on Thanksgiving for years."

"I see," Sal says with an understanding nod. "The Raiders suck worse than the Cowboys, by the way."

"How does it feel to have a team that plays in New Jersey named after New York?" she asks.

"Touché," he says. It is hard being a Jets fan.

"You will enjoy the haunted house," she says firmly, returning to the original conversation. "And if you give me any more trouble I will most definitely not wear the slutty librarian costume when we get back to my place."

"I didn't realize that was a costume," he says with a grin, and inches the car forward.

Twenty minutes later, much sooner than Sal had expected, they turn into the parking area for "Dr. Venom's House of Horrors." In spite of the cheesy name, Sal has heard that this one is much better than the plethora of similar attractions that spring up every October, all promising chills, thrills, and more terror than the human heart can stand. The real terror is how much they charge for admission. This place probably rakes in more cash in one month than the bookstore does in a year. Perhaps it's a side business he should look into.

More shocking than the price, though, is the fact that the "House of Horrors" really is a house. Typically these things were held in vacant warehouses or at strip malls in spaces once occupied by K-Mart or Circuit City. But this is an actual house, two-story, wraparound porch upstairs and down, most likely built in the 1920s. It is surrounded by retail and commercial development, the last holdout in the area, but it seems well-maintained, at least on the outside. Despite this, and in spite of the bank of floodlights illuminating the parking area, Sal feels a sudden chill that has nothing to do with the wind.

Outside the house several booths are set up, much like what you would see in any traveling carnival. Sal immediately starts toward the nearest one, but Julia steers him toward the entrance of the house instead.

"Let's not have a repeat of our last experience with carnies," she says sweetly. "I don't think you can afford it."

Near the front door he hands two twenties to a young woman dressed as a vampire...if vampires were porn stars, that is. She takes the money, hands them two tickets, and automatically starts into a canned spiel, one she has clearly given hundreds of times already, in the worst Transylvanian accent he can imagine.

"Dr. Venom's House of Horrors is a self-guided supernatural experience. Simply follow the lights on the floor throughout the house – or the screams if the lights go out – and you will eventually come out at this same entry point, if you return at all. The entire house is open for exploration, including the upstairs, except for rooms where the door is locked. Those rooms are off limits."

"Why?" Julia asks.

The little vampire blinks rapidly several times, unaccustomed to having her well-rehearsed speech interrupted.

"Um, because the family hasn't cleared those out yet," she says, recovering her voice, which is much higher-pitched now that she is off script. "They're in the process of selling the house following the death of the owner, and are making a little extra money by letting us put on Dr. Venom's here."

"More like a ton of money," Sal mutters. Julia shushes him.

"I see," Julia says. "Please continue with your introduction."

The girl blinks some more, then falls back into character and that dreadful accent. "You will encounter numerous ghosts, ghouls, and monsters on your journey tonight, but they are not allowed, by law, to touch you, and we ask that you not touch any of them."

"If they touch me I will shoot them," Sal says in a better accent than hers.

"No firearms allowed," she replies, remaining in character this time.

"No sign posted saying that," he retorts. "Have to have one of those to stop me...by law."

Before the little vamp can argue further, Julia pushes Sal through the front door and into a dimly lit entryway.

"You can be such a pain in the ass sometimes," she says. But Sal can tell she's smiling.

For all the terrifying potential promised by the house itself and the ominous declarations of the young vampire, Sal is decidedly unimpressed. There is the natural spookiness of a big, dark old house at night, and the screams of the patrons scattered throughout the house occasionally add a chilling effect, but most of the "scares" are actually nothing more than "startles." When a 300-pound guy in a werewolf mask leaps out from a dark corner, you're going to jump, but not from fear, especially once you read "Harrison's Hardware" on his T-shirt. Apparently he either couldn't afford the entire Wolfman suit or was too big to fit into it.

All of the usual props are here, of course: there are bowls full of peeled grapes meant to look like extracted eyeball, severed mannequin limbs covered liberally with red dye-infused corn syrup, and a sound effects CD blasting from strategically placed speakers that Sal is sure he had as a kid...on vinyl. All in all, an amateurish setup in his opinion, and nowhere near worth twenty bucks a person.

Julia, however, is completely into the experience, digging her nails into his arm at the slightest sound and screaming like a teenager at every turn. When the hockey mask wearing, fake chainsaw wielding lunatic appears at the bottom of the stairs Sal fears she may actually faint. Instead she lets out a scream so loud it startles the lunatic, and as he steps back from them she seizes Sal's hand and they bolt up to the second floor.

This floor is more sparsely decorated, as if Dr. Venom ran low on cash when it came time to deck out the upstairs. Only one door is open; inside a mad scientist works on a screaming girl strapped to a hospital gurney. A bluish haze drifts around the girl's head, and it takes a moment in the dim light for Sal realize that between screams she is taking drags from a cigarette. Now he wants one.

He is about to suggest they leave when he catches sight of a figure at the end of the hallway. It is an old man in an immaculate gray suit, totally out of place here. The man crooks a bony finger, beckoning Sal toward him. Sal pulls Julia, who was transfixed by the smoking girl for some odd reason, down the hall behind him. When they reach the man he points at a closed door.

"Would you like to see the library?" he asks, his voice a rich baritone.

"Absolutely," Sal replies. Finally something cool: a haunted library. He tries the doorknob but it does not turn. "It's locked," Sal says, disappointed.

"It will open for you, bookman," the old gentleman says with a slight smile. He moves his hand close to the knob and the door springs open.

"Cool trick," Julia says as they enter, and Sal receives his first real shock of the night.

He had expected either walls painted to resemble books on shelves, like the props from a Broadway play, or maybe a few small bookcases filled with Readers Digest Condensed Books, the kind you buy by the foot for decoration. He had pictured dust and fake cobwebs and perhaps a gaunt figure at a desk, like a scene from *The Raven* come to life, or maybe even a "body" on the floor with a bloody candlestick near the head.

What he did not expect was what he actually sees: he is standing inside a real library, with built-in, floor-to-ceiling oak bookcases ringing the room. Whereas the rest of the house is in shadow, here the space is bathed in light, which reflects softly off a sea of leather bound books that are most assuredly not simply decorations. He gazes around the room in wonder.

"I don't get it," Julia says, breaking the silence. "It's a library. What's scary about that?"

The old man nods; in the better lighting Sal notices small tufts of white hair sprouting from his large ears.

"This, my dear girl," the man says so softly she has to lean toward him to hear, "may well be the most terrifying room in this house tonight. Not because of monsters or screams or decorations, but because of what will happen to these books if no one intervenes.

Sal seems not to have heard him, moving away from Julia to examine the shelves. He takes a book down and opens it: *Candide* by Voltaire. The leather binding is not original to this edition. He takes several more and examines them; someone has rebound every book in this library.

"These are gorgeous," Sal says. "The leather on these covers is hand-tooled. Simply amazing work." The old man brightens at this compliment.

"Indeed," he replies. "The late owner was a cobbler, actually a boot maker, by trade. He knew how to work leather, and he loved his books. So in his later years he married his two passions to produce this." He makes a sweeping gesture with his arm.

"A lot of these are first editions," Sal observes, flipping through more of the books. "With modern firsts the dust jackets are crucial to collectors. He threw away 90% of the resale value when he replaced the dust jackets with leather."

"But did he really, my boy?" the man asks, gazing intently at Sal. "A fast-buck artist might think so, but do you?"

Sal traces his finger over the gilt-stamped spine of *An Appointment in Samara*. No paper cover, regardless of how iconic the artwork, was ever this beautiful.

"No," he says, and the man nods in agreement.

"What did you mean when you said something terrifying will happen to them?" Julia asks, moving closer to Sal. The man seems friendly enough, yet he also makes her more uneasy than any of the frights downstairs.

"His children, his heirs, had the books appraised after he died," the man explains. "The appraiser came to the same conclusion your young man did at first: with the original covers gone the books are essentially worthless monetarily, at least to most collectors. The best offer they received was from a recycler who will strip the leather off and pulp the paper."

Sal turns away from the shelves, aghast at what the man just said. "How much did he offer them?" he asks. "It can't have been much."

"Two hundred dollars and he hauls the lot away for them. They didn't want to have to carry them downstairs."

"Two hundred dollars? That's less than fifty cents a book," Sal says, making a quick scan around the room. "That is insane. Think of the time, effort, and skill that went into rebinding all of these books. I know a few collectors who would pay handsomely for some of these simply for their beauty."

"The late owner's children are not, sadly, book lovers," the man replies, a hint of bitterness in his tone.

Sal makes a quick decision, one he really should talk to Camden about first. But the gleaming burgundy cover of *Crime and Punishment* convinces him that Jacob will back him on this, and Camden trusts Jacob implicitly when it comes to old books.

"Tell the heirs I will pay them two thousand dollars cash and move the books for them," he says. "Don't tell them they're worth ten times that amount."

Julia jabs him in the side, her eyes wide. He ignores her and removes a business card from his wallet. He tries to hand it to the man, but he does not take it.

"You can tell them yourself," he says. He is smiling now, looking quite relieved. "His daughter is working at the concession stand downstairs – making sure she gets her proper cut of the sales, no doubt – and his son is dressed as ridiculously overweight Wolfman."

Sal looks around the room again, marveling at how close these books came to being lost forever. He turns back to the man to ask how he knew the old owner, but before he can say a word he slips through the door into the hall and is gone.

The next morning Sal, Julia, and Ramon are back at the house, which appears far less ominous in the daylight. It had taken all of ten seconds for the heirs, who were clearly more greedy than bright, to break their deal with the recycler and accept Sal's offer instead. As they carefully pack the final boxes of books, a photograph slips from one of them, a copy of Shakespeare's sonnets bound in black leather. Sal kneels down, picks it up, and stares at it. When he lingers in that position, Julia peers over his shoulder.

The photo is years, perhaps decades old, and shows a tall, distinguished gentleman with his arm around a plain but attractive woman of about the same age. In the background is one of these very bookcases, but only half of the volumes in the picture are leather bound; the rest are in their original state, with paper dustcovers.

"Who is this?" Sal asks the daughter, whose name is Kay or Kate or something like that; he hadn't been paying much attention when she introduced herself the previous evening, so focused was he on the books.

"Oh, that's my parents," she says in a surprisingly unsentimental tone. "You can keep it if you want. I suppose his picture should stay with his books."

"This is your late father?" Sal asks, exchanging a confused look with Julia.

"Yep," Kay or Kate answers. "With mom and his silly books." She follows Ramon downstairs as he leaves with the last box.

Sal looks from Julia to the photograph in his hand again. The man is certainly younger, but the gray suit is the same, as are the piercing eyes and even the hint of hair starting to sprout from the overly large ears. It is their guide from the previous night, a gentleman who would not allow even death to keep him from protecting his beloved books.

17

"The Chronicles of Luis Ortiz"

Max is sitting at a corner table in The Daily Grind, trying in vain to turn an idea not even worthy of a short story into a novella. As interesting as all of the people who work at The Last Word are, he cannot find a story compelling enough to tie them all together. He had first thought he might just write a book about the store itself and the lunatics that work there, but who would ever read something like that?

He is about to give up and go back to the store when Ortiz walks in. Ortiz intrigues him, and not just because as a writer interesting people always intrigue him. There is something about this guy, something he can't really put his finger on, something that makes him the gravitational center of any room he is in.

He is thinking these things when Ortiz turns and makes eye contact with him. A grin spreads across his face, or rather spreads wider, as he always seems to be smiling, no matter what is going on around him. The night they changed the price stickers at Discount Books is a perfect example.

Looking back it was a miracle that they had pulled the thing off at all, let alone as quickly as they did, but whereas the rest of them had been furiously pulling down books and affixing the new stickers, Ortiz had moved at a pace that could only be described as languid, singing a Spanish folk song as he went. Yet he somehow managed to complete two shelves for every one Max did.

Ortiz moves fluidly to the table for a man of his size and takes a seat. He is truly a compelling figure, well over six feet tall and at least 250 pounds with not a bit of fat evident. He has light blue eyes that sparkle when he speaks, and his voice is melodious; his English is excellent, though heavily accented. Max has also noticed that for some reason he never uses contractions. The slight gray at the temples of his short black hair puts him in his early 40s, but he has the unlined face of someone ten years younger.

"Good morning, Maximilian," he says cheerily. "How are you this fine day? I have just completed a five-mile run and sauna and am ready to relax. It was an excellent run; I ran like the wing-sandaled god Mercury."

Ran like the wing-sandaled god Mercury? Max thinks. Who talks like this? He doesn't comment on that, though, but rather on something more tangible.

"Max is short for Maxwell," he says politely, having had to explain this many times during his life. Ortiz nods and smiles even more.

"Perhaps," he says. "But Maximilian is a name with gravitas, and you are a man with gravitas. Thus I will call you Maximilian."

Coming from anyone else, this declaration would be preposterous. Yet from Ortiz is seems as normal as saying that water is wet. Max can't bring himself to protest a even little.

"How goes the quest for the Great American Novel?" Ortiz asks as the waitress sets his coffee and scone down on the table. Interesting that everyone else has to walk to the counter when their order is ready, yet his is delivered.

"It's slow, tedious, and frustrating," he answers honestly. "I thought I would be able to write about the people at the bookstore, but that's just not working, maybe because it's been done so much better before."

"Better before?" Ortiz repeats, consuming half of the scone in one bite.

"Many times," Max says. "The best was probably Sylvia Beach's memoir *Shakespeare and Company*, though that wasn't fiction. There are entire mystery series set in bookstores, and a number of others where bookstores are a key part of the story. I can't find a way to make it fresh."

"I am sure you will find a way," Ortiz says. It does not come out as encouragement, but rather as a plain fact. "You are a teller of tales, a chronicler. Salvatore loaned me

187

a few of your novels; I enjoyed them very much. You have a keen eye for things others would overlook, which is what makes you an excellent chronicler."

"You keep calling me a chronicler," Max says, intrigued. "But chronicles are traditionally true stories. A bit embellished perhaps, depending on the subject, but still true."

Ortiz sets down his cup and the smile vanishes. This is the most serious expression Max had ever seen cross his face.

"All stories are true, my friend," he says. "You may call them fiction, but at their core they are all as true as if they had been documentaries. And if you tell the tale well enough, it becomes true in the reader's mind, which makes it as real as the table we are sitting at now."

"I can agree with that in theory –" Max starts to say.

"It is not theory, it is reality," Ortiz continues, cutting him off. "Let me give you an example, and though it is from film, the film began life as a great novel. I was a young boy when I saw *The Godfather* for the first time, and because I do not have your gift of language the effect it had on me cannot be described. Suffice it to say it impacted my worldview completely. I have seen the film many, many times, hundreds at least, and each time I still weep when Santino is killed on the causeway. I pray each time I watch it that Don Vito – a great man – will not be deceived by Barzini. Each time I see the film I become part of their world, and they become part of mine."

"I understand that a film or a novel can have a deep effect on a person," Max agrees.

"It is so much more than that, though," Ortiz says. "When I say it becomes real, becomes a part of a person's reality, I mean it in more than a symbolic way. People of faith will sometimes use the phrase 'What Would Jesus Do'. For me it has always been 'What Would the Corleones Do?'

"I have a number of cousins in Granada and Madrid," he continues, the change of subject catching Max off guard. "My mother was from Spain – it is from her I received my blue eyes – and she had many brothers and sisters. Some of these cousins I have met, and others I have not, but without debate they are all real, no?"

"I would say so, sure," Max replies.

"Yet I have spent far more time with the Corleones over the course of my life, know them better, and have been influenced more by them than by any of my Spanish relations except for my dear mother. What began as fiction was transformed into reality."

Ortiz's seriousness melts away as quickly as it had appeared, the smile returning to its usual brightness.

"That was one of the best arguments in defense of fiction I've ever heard," Max says. "Have you ever considered writing yourself?"

Ortiz shakes his head and finishes off the scone.

"I am no writer, Maximilian," he says. "Writers possess the unique magical ability to bring the events of our existence to life; I do not posses this gift. My gift is to live life in a manner which will someday compel a writer to tell my story to future generations. Odysseus had Homer, Jesus had the gospel writers, Michael Corleone had Puzo and Coppola. Sadly, thus far I have not found my chronicler. It is possible he will appear after I am gone, but I hope not."

Max is not sure which is more amazing: the fact that Ortiz lumped Odysseus, Jesus, and Michael Corleone together as is they were of equal importance in human history, or that he actually believes that someday people will write stories about him. It is a fine line between self-confidence and megalomania. Still, as he considers this behemoth across the table from him he thinks it probably will happen someday. And then an idea occurs to him, the kind people think writers get all the time but in reality are as infrequent as snow in summer.

"Let me write your story," he says, surprising even himself as the words come out.

Ortiz does not appear to be shocked by the suggestion, but neither does he respond immediately. He places his elbows on the table and tents his hands in front of him. His silence continues almost to the point of being awkward before he finally speaks.

"A most intriguing suggestion," he says. "I certainly have enough experiences to fill many volumes, and I am confident that you would do a most excellent job as my chronicler."

"But?" Max prods.

"Ah, yes, the inevitable 'but.' As I am sure you have surmised, I have both past and ongoing activities that fall outside of the short-sighted and arbitrary laws of this and other countries."

"The possibility had crossed my mind, yes," Max says with a laugh. It also occurred to him that he could use Lou's dialogue verbatim in any book he wrote about him.

"This being the case," Ortiz says, "there are certain details that would have to be significantly altered, if not removed entirely. I fear this could dampen the impact of the tale."

"You would be surprised at how well I can alter details to disguise actual events," Max assures him. "Besides, I have something in mind that will confuse even the most keen-eyed law enforcement officer with an interest in you." Like his initial idea to write about Ortiz, this idea has just now come to him.

This immediately piques Luis's interest and he leans across the table.

"My story told through the eyes of a samurai who travels to ancient Rome and with wisdom, guile and the favor of the gods becomes emperor, perhaps?" he suggests. "I have seen this in my dreams many times."

"Uh, let's save that one for later," Max says, though it is definitely an interesting idea. "I'm thinking of something more along the lines of making you a private investigator. I've written quite a few crime stories lately and I rather like the genre. Making you the so-called 'good guy' would throw off those pesky investigators."

Ortiz laughs loudly and snaps his fingers in a rhythm that puts Max in mind of a 1930s Cuban band leader. He clearly loves the idea.

"An inspired suggestion!" he exclaims. "We must ask my brother Jake if he will consent to being my partner in the books. He could be Hawk to *my* Spenser; it will do him good to see the world as a minority for a change. How soon can we begin?"

"We already have," Max says, jotting down notes in his journal. He can already see the outline of the first book in his head.

"Excellent," Ortiz says with a nod. "We shall meet for dinner tonight at Ignatio's Steakhouse on 7th Street to discuss this project further. I will invite Jake and we will feast like the kings of old."

He stands, claps Max hard on the shoulder, and strides out of the coffee shop without another word, a small group of people near the door parting like the Red Sea to allow him through.

As he writes this down the line, *feast like the kings of old,* in his journal, Max marvels at the serendipity of their meeting this morning, one that could have been completely missed had he decided to leave only a few minutes earlier. As he packs up his things to leave, he also wonders, if only fleetingly, what exactly he has gotten himself into.

18

"The Silver-Haired Sirens Book Club"

In the time since Sal and Camden have taken ownership of The Last Word the number of reading groups that either meet at or have been formed through the store has grown from zero to more than thirty. They range from a group of older men seriously studying Russian literature (organized by Jacob, of course) to a Lost Generation club (led by Heather) to a super-secret trashy romance group that Camden attends. Sal is convinced that the majority use the groups as an excuse to sit around drinking wine, but as long as they buy their books from the store he tries not to judge.

The newest group, much to Jacob's chagrin, was started by his wife Esther, and tonight they are meeting at his house. He had hoped to work late and avoid being home, but it is Sunday and the store closed at 6:00. Now, rather than enjoying the peace and quiet of his Rare Books Room, he has been pressed into service as little more than a glorified butler, bringing the ladies canapés and refilling their wine glasses. Adding insult to injury, Esther's sisters

Sarah and Miriam are both visiting from Arizona. Again. On the plus side, they prepared most of the food while he was at work.

As septuagenarian women begin arriving, Jacob scurries from kitchen to front door to living room, doing the job of three people at once. His sisters-in-law are perched on either side of his wife on the leather sofa, determinedly not lifting a finger to help him. In his mind he begins plotting a revenge scenario worthy of Dostoyevsky.

When the last lady has arrived, handed Jacob her coat, and settled in with a glass of Merlot, Esther places a copy of the novel they have all just read in the center of the coffee table. For a group of elderly women, their choice of books is quire eclectic. This time it is the story of a young man's journey from destitute elephant herder to Prime Minister of Bangladesh, and the Australian expatriate gunrunner who steals his heart. The author is a twenty year old prodigy from Croatia, and the novel is called, for reasons that escape Jacob, *Mango*.

"Thank you all for being here," Esther says. "The Silver-Haired Sirens Book Club will now come to order." She is very organized, running the book group like a meeting of the Elks Lodge. For his part, Jacob wishes he had never mentioned that the part-time female employees of the store were collectively called The Sirens.

Now that the actual meeting has started, Jacob considers retreating to the safety of the kitchen, perhaps reading a little Pasternak until his services are required again. But as he watches his wife take control of the proceedings he finds himself transfixed by her. This is nothing new; she has amazed and mesmerized him for nearly 50 years.

Jacob was a graduate student at the University of Chicago studying, naturally, Russian Literature, when he first met Esther Shapiro in, of all places, and all-night Laundromat. He had been alone, he thought, and was standing inside the tub of a washing machine trying to pack just a few more clothes into the thing in order to not have to use a second one; he was a poor student and money was tight. He had just wedged the last shirt under the rim of the tub when someone spoke behind him.

"You really should separate your colors," the voice said. "They'll never get clean jammed in like that. There's barely room for the water."

He turned, still standing in the machine, and saw the most beautiful creature he had ever laid eyes on: flowing hair darker than charcoal, deep brown eyes, and a halo around her head. The halo turned out to be a streetlight shining through the plate glass window behind her, but she was an angel just the same.

That was the effect Esther Shapiro had on him the first time they met, and the effect was undiminished through five decades of marriage (he had proposed only 17 days after the night at the Laundromat), two children (who rarely visited, ungrateful rats), and the surliness that was his natural disposition. Her hair was indeed silver now, so the name of the book club was fitting, but her eyes were as clear and beautiful as the first night he had gotten lost in them.

Miriam and Sarah are shouting now, rousing Jacob from his pleasant remembrance. Esther could control an infantry division if she wanted to, but had always been slow reigning in her sisters. They were older, and either out of respect or the knowledge that it was a losing battle she gave them latitude that few others enjoyed.

"That's not true!" Miriam exclaims. "The gunrunner was not a man. Her name was Tracy."

"How many female gunrunners have you ever heard of?" Sarah retorts. "He was most certainly a man."

"The author never uses the word 'he' when talking about her," Miriam insists.

"Nor does he use the word 'she' when talking about *him*," Sarah counters.

Esther holds up her hand, and to Jacob's surprise they both fall silent. Perhaps in this one area they defer to her because she has a degree from DePaul, which means something in Chicago. A nice Jewish girl with a degree from a Catholic college; she is full of contradictions.

"I think," Esther says, her hand still raised, "that the author purposely left the gunrunner's gender ambiguous, right down to a name that can be either male or female." Jacob has not read the book and does not care if the character Tracy is a man, a woman, or a potted plant. He is marveling at Esther's raised hand, the skin of which is as smooth as a baby's; his, by contrast, is as wrinkled as a pug's face.

"But why leave something so important ambiguous?" asks June, a spry widow they know from synagogue. She had been the one who suggested *Mango* to the group.

"Precisely because it is so important," Esther replies, finally lowering her hand. "I believe he is making the point that their love is what matters, regardless of nationality or social standing or even gender. He writes the characters, and the story, in such a way that you can choose whatever interpretation you are most comfortable with, which is refreshingly inclusive."

There are murmurs around the room, mostly of agreement, but Jacob is unconvinced. He likes his characters to be easily identifiable.

"Unless you are really analyzing the text, like my sisters," Esther continues, "the story flows without this becoming a distraction. It took a lot of skill to stay as gender-neutral as he did."

"Like the way Melissa Etheridge wrote her early songs," says Marcy.

Everyone turns to look at her. At 80 years old, she is the senior woman in the reading group, but you would never know this from her taste in clothes, music, and men.

"My granddaughter gave me her greatest hits CD after my cancer scare," Marcy explains, "because of her song 'I Run for Life.' She's a lesbian, you know."

"Your granddaughter?" June asks, shocked. "I thought she was married to that nice podiatrist."

"Not my granddaughter," Marcy sighs. "Melissa Etheridge."

"Not that there's anything wrong with that," Miriam and Sarah say in unison, and then dissolve into a fit of childish laughter. They are addicted to the television show *Seinfeld*, and quote it whenever possible. Jacob never understood the show's popularity; a show about nothing was like a novel with no plot.

Prompted by Marcy's mention of her granddaughter, the discussion veers away from the book to everyone's family, the difficulty finding good kosher meat in Texas, and the latest news on who had what life-threatening illness. Jacob refills several empty wineglasses, realizing in that moment that, for all the trouble they can be, he prefers the company of the young people at the bookshop to that of people his own age. If they don't exactly keep him young, they at least help him forget that he is old.

Before the evening gets too late, Esther wrestles the conversation back to books. They have to choose the next one they will read, and she has been pondering this for some time.

"I had originally thought we should go with something light after the complexity of *Mango*," she says to the ladies. "Perhaps one of Nick Hornby's early novels."

"Oh, I just love him," Marcy says.

"However," Esther continues, and Marcy's face falls, "we have a unique opportunity right now that may never present itself again."

This grabs everyone's attention. At their respective ages, unique opportunities are difficult to find.

"As some of you may know," Esther says, "the author Max Luther is the first Writer in Residence at Jacob's bookstore." Jacob smiles at the way she calls it *his* bookstore. "And from what Jacob tells me the man is liable to vanish as suddenly as he appeared. I suggest we read one of his novels in the hope that he will still be here when we finish and might agree to come speak to us about the book."

There are murmurs of approval from around the room. Having a real, live author speak to them would be quite a coup, one they could brag about to their friends at the beauty parlor.

"I saw him typing on an old manual typewriter in front of the store a few days ago," Marcy says. "He's very sexy. Older than I typically like them, but still very sexy."

"But would he come talk to a bunch of old ladies?" Miriam asks. "He's famous, sort of."

They turn in unison to Jacob, the unspoken request hanging in the air. He has no idea if Max will agree to this, but he also doesn't want to disappoint everyone.

"I think he would," Jacob says. "He seems a very agreeable person to me." *When he's not falling down drunk with Sal*, he thinks.

"Excellent," Esther says. "I think we should avoid *Liquid Time*. I imagine everyone asks him about that one, and probably the same with *Midnight in Trafalgar Square*. Perhaps one of the lesser known novels."

She produces a small notebook as if from thin air and flips to the middle. Jacob suppresses a smile; his wife is the queen of all note-takers. She has more journals, notebooks, and diaries than he has books. Someone could write an extremely detailed biography of Esther from the amount of material she will leave behind.

"I jotted down a few of his titles with the publisher's blurb for each one," she says. "The reviews on this one were mixed, but I think *Cable Car Memories* would be a good choice for our group. Jacob can order a copy for everyone from the store, with his staff discount as usual, of course."

"Fine with me," Miriam says, "as long as you can tell the male characters from the female."

Everyone laughs heartily at this, everyone except Jacob. He realizes in an instant that this simple comment means that his sisters-in-law's visit, and his own personal hell, has just been extended for a least two more weeks. He foresees some long nights at the bookshop in his immediate future.

19

"Max Moves On"

Eventually the worm turns for everyone, and it is during a dinner of take-out Chinese that Max informs Sal and Camden that it has finally, quite unexpectedly, turned for him. Sal has just speared a chunk of Moo Shu Pork when Max says, quite out of the blue, that he will be moving out of their apartment in the next few days. Sal drops the chopstick into the cardboard container.

"You're leaving?" he asks. "Why?"

"I figured you'd be glad to be rid of me," he says with a smile in Camden's direction. "If I'm going to stay down here, and it looks like I am, then it's time I found a place of my own, which I have."

"How will you afford it?" Sal asks. "Did you get a royalty check or something?"

"Even better than that," Max says, popping a snow pea into his mouth. "My agent tracked me down with some very good news."

"I thought you had fired your agent," Camden says, confused. "Or that he had fired you. During your talk that day you said you'd had several agents and that they were all blood-sucking parasites."

"That is as true now as ever," Max says. "And this one, who is actually a woman, had indeed fired me. What we both forgot was that long before getting fed up with my lack of production, she had pitched *Midnight in Trafalgar Square* to several movie producers. Things in Hollywood move pretty slowly, and she just now heard back from one of them. Since she pitched it, and since there is now a percentage to be taken, she's decided I'm her client again."

"They're paying you to write a screenplay?" Sal asks.

"Even better, my friend. They are paying me for the rights to make the book into a film. I may help with the screenplay, but that will cost them extra. This is basically money for something I already did a long time ago."

"How much did they pay, if you don't mind me asking?" Camden inquires. "Depending on where you live, even down here rents can be expensive. Not like London or New York, but still pricey if your income is, shall we say, haphazard."

"I like the way you phrased that," he says, taking a swig of Shiner. "Can I steal that line?"

"Sure," she says, pleased with the compliment.

"I don't usually like talking about the money side of things – so mercenary – but it is more than enough for me to live comfortably for at least a year, maybe two, down here even if I don't work on the screen play. That's more cushion than I've had since before my first divorce."

"Where did you find a place?" Sal asks in a sullen tone. Camden thinks he is afraid his hero and new playmate will be moving too far away for him to skip out on work to drink, which in her opinion would not be such a bad thing.

"I found a nice loft on the far south side of downtown," Max says. "The part you said was sketchy now but would improve as the gentrification moved that way."

Sal brightens at this news. Max will still be in walking distance, though it will be a pretty long walk. Maybe he'll use one of those rent-a-bike things that have been popping up lately. Much easier than finding parking.

"Also, as much as I've enjoyed it," Max says hesitantly, "I'll have to give up my position as Writer in Residence. I recently figured out my next novel - or novels, it's looking like a series – and since I'll have money to eat now I'm going to work on that full-time." He does not mention that Ortiz will be his main character; if Luis wants to tell them he can.

"So if we've lost our Writer in Residence," she says. "Does that mean the end of the project?"

Sal shakes his head. The idea is bigger than one writer, even one he likes and admires as much as Max.

"No," he says firmly. "I think it should continue. Plenty of local writers need exposure, and we can give them that."

"Agreed," she says. It had been one of his better ideas, certainly the most normal, and she wants to encourage normal as much as possible.

"I'd be glad to help you find someone," Max says. "I take my status as the first-ever one seriously. It was quite the honor."

"The best part was still you scaring the hell out of Cam that first morning," Sal says. "No one who comes after you will ever be able to top that."

"You're a funny man, Terranova," she says. "A very funny man."

True to his word, Max arrives early on the morning they will be interviewing for his replacement, both wide awake and sober. Julia wrote an ad that ran for two weeks in the local free arts paper, *Fort Worth Now*, as well as on multiple writing websites. They were inundated with applications, even though Max's successor would not have the luxury of sleeping on their couch. Rather, they had set up a cot in the basement with the used books. Camden sincerely hoped that whoever they chose would already have a place to live.

Sal is fine with someone living in the basement, but is not looking forward to an entire day of interviews. The last time they had done this, when looking for a new staff person after taking over the store, had been an absolute beating. But it was how they had found Heather, so he supposed it had been well worth the trouble.

Max has only ever interviewed people in connection with books he was working on, so this is a completely new experience for him. He finds out just how new with the first applicant.

"So tell us about your literary idols," Sal asks the woman, who could easily have been one of the Sirens.

"I really admire Dan Brown and James Patterson," she says enthusiastically. "I just love the way they can tell a story without using a bunch of big words."

Sal looks from Camden to Max, then down at the woman's application.

"On your application you said you love the classics," Sal says.

"Well wouldn't you consider *Angels and Demons* a classic?" the woman replies. Sal thanks her and says they will be in touch, then sets her application on fire with his Zippo.

The next four candidates are variations on the same theme: Dan Brown disciples, post-apocalyptic vampire serialists, even one who was rewriting all of Shakespeare's plays as detective novels since they are in the public domain and lack copyright protection. Sal is indignant about this last one, but Max jots down a note to himself to find out if this is something he might try as well.

Applicant number six is a young woman named Mariel; Max recognizes her as having been at his talk on the writing life. He had thought she was around 16 years old then, but according to her application she is 22. Funny how they look younger as he gets older.

"Tell us about your literary idols," Sal asks for the sixth time that morning, praying he will receive a different answer from the ones he's gotten so far.

"In no particular order," Mariel says, "Mary Shelley, Dante, Hunter S. Thompson, and Shirley Jackson."

Max and Sal stare at her, speechless. Camden leans over and whispers in Sal's ear.

"Is that good? The only name I recognize is Dante." He shushes her.

"*Frankenstein, The Inferno, Fear and Loathing in Las Vegas,* and *The Haunting of Hill House*," Max says. "So you like your strange, scary stories with a literary edge."

Mariel nods.

"You understand that this isn't a position that pays what a full-time job would," Camden tells her.

"I have a job working nights at UPS," she replies. "Though I would consider leaving that if you had an opening for a bookseller."

"That might be possible," Sal says, though the idea of this girl and Heather joining forces is more than a little scary.

"And you live nearby?" Camden continues, ignoring Sal's willingness to add more to their payroll.

"I live with my sister and her husband off Camp Bowie Blvd.," she says.

"Another Shirley Jackson connection," Max muses.

"No," Mariel corrects him. "I actually like them."

"Are you currently working on something?" Sal asks.

"Yes," she says, her demeanor brightening. "I'm 400 pages into the second draft of a novel."

The three of them look at each other and nod; this is the one they are looking for.

"I think you are exactly the kind of person we're looking for to succeed Mr. Luther," Camden says. "And as an added perk, he has agreed to act as a mentor if you would like."

"That would be great!" she says, but then her thrilled expression fades.

"I have something I should tell you," she says softly. "In case you do a background check or something."

Shit, Sal thinks. *She's got a record.* As long as it's not drugs or animal cruelty he's pretty sure he can talk Camden into hiring her anyway. He is certainly not one to throw stones at someone with past interactions with the law.

"I was arrested a few years ago in Illinois," she says. "It's part of the reason I moved here. I wasn't convicted, and if it had happened in Texas I probably wouldn't have even been charged. But it's out there."

"What happened, dear?" Camden asks.

"I was out writing late one night in a park near where I lived," she says. "My mom kept telling me it wasn't safe to be in parks that late, but with what I write the darkness inspires me. Anyway, a guy came up and demanded that I give him my purse. I refused, and he pulled out a knife."

Camden gasps when she says this, and she stops talking. Sal pats Camden on the back and nods for Mariel to continue.

"The guy called me some ugly names," Mariel says, "and then he lunged at me with the knife. He was kind of off balance — I think he'd been drinking — and he missed me. He recovered and was about to try again, but before he could I stabbed him if the eye with my fountain pen."

"Did he die?" Sal asks, fairly sure he already knows the answer.

"Yes," Mariel says. "A few days later."

"Sounds like a clear case of self-defense to me," Max says. "I can't believe they even arrested you."

"They might not have," she says, "if not for the fact that in the heat of the moment, with the adrenaline pumping, I looked down at him while he was writhing around on the ground and said: '*The pen is mightier than the sword, motherfucker.*' An old couple walking their dog heard me and told the police, who tried to make it into a something, because obviously a nice girl wouldn't be in the park after dark and wouldn't instinctively drive a pen into a guy's brain."

"Fucking cops," Sal mutters.

"We would never hold something like that against you," Camden says after a moment. "You had every right to defend yourself. I'm glad you weren't hurt."

"And it could make a hell of a story someday," Max says. "When you feel comfortable writing it."

"So I've still got the job?" she asks.

"No," Sal says, and her shoulders slump. "You do not have the *job*, because it is not a job. It is a position of great honor and prestige. And we would be thrilled if you would accept it."

Mariel blinks rapidly several times, and for a minute Sal is afraid she is going to cry. How can someone who killed a guy with a pen cry over getting a low-paying writing gig? She does not cry however; instead she lets out a shriek of triumph, jumps up, and kisses Max full on the mouth. He does not seem to mind one bit. Very volatile, those writers.

20

"The Lost Manuscript"

Sal drags himself downstairs late the next morning to find Jacob Weinberg in an animated conversation with Charles Moriarty, the owner of Moriarty & Sons Booksellers. A much younger man stands off to one side of them, stifling a yawn and clearly wishing he was somewhere else. His gray eyes and the shape of his nose make it unmistakable that he is a relative of Moriarty's, but whether a son or grandson Sal has no clue. He walks over to the group and catches the end of what Jacob is saying.

"I've known you for decades, Charles," Jacob says with more emotion than was typical for him. "And I've heard this story a hundred times. But, with all due respect to your family history, I just don't believe that book exists."

"What book?" Sal asks before Charles has a chance to respond. The two older men turn to look at him, surprised by the interruption. The younger man's expression changes as well. He stares at Sal with wide-eyed recognition.

"You're Sally Fingers!" he exclaims.

Sal studies him more closely before answering. He is in his early twenties, barely old enough to drink, wearing a Blink-182 T-shirt and ripped Levis that are, thankfully, not sagging. Unless Charles waited until very late in life to have children, this kid is his grandson.

"Just Sal," Sal says with a nod to the boy.

"But I saw a show that said -"

"I was in Altoona that night," Sal says, cutting him off.

"Atlantic City!" a voice yells from across the room. "Why can you never get that right?"

Sal waves at Julia, who smiles and goes back to sorting books; he hadn't even realized she was there.

"Right, Atlantic City." He turns to Jacob. "You were saying something about a book not existing."

"My old friend here," Jacob says with a wave toward Charles, "has bought into an old family legend about a book that simply cannot be true."

"It's true," Charles Moriarty says softly. "And it does exist."

"Have you ever seen it?" Jacob demands. Charles is silent. "That's what I thought. It's as crazy as believing that wild story about Lucky Luciano writing a novel in prison. Even Sal wouldn't believe that one."

He turns to Sal for confirmation, but Sal simply smiles. There are only a handful of people who know that Lucky's novel actually does exist, and fewer still who know that it is sitting on Sal's bookshelf upstairs at this very moment.

"Mr. Moriarty," he says. "What is the name of this book you're talking about?"

"It is called *Garibaldi and Lee*," Charles replies. "And it's not actually a book per se, but rather an original handwritten manuscript."

"Never heard of it," Sal says. "Who was the author?"

Charles hesitates for a moment and glances at Jacob as if he is now unsure about answering.

"Tell him," Jacob says. "He'll definitely agree with me once you do."

"There are actually two authors, Mr. Terranova," he says after some hesitation.

"Ok," Sal says. "What two authors? Would I have heard of them?"

"Most certainly," Charles replies. "*Garibaldi and Lee* was a collaboration between Charles Dickens and Alexandre Dumas."

The young man shuffles his feet uneasily; he has obviously heard this many times before. Jacob smiles at his old friend a little sadly. Sal stands there, waiting for the punch line, but none comes.

"Charles Dickens and Alexandre Dumas?" he repeats. "As in *Great Expectations* and *The Three Musketeers*?"

"The very same," Charles says, relieved that Sal did not burst out laughing.

"You're going to need to explain this to me," Sal says, causing Jacob to arch a bushy white eyebrow in surprise.

"You can't actually believe…" Jacob begins.

"I don't believe anything yet," Sal cuts him off. "But I owe this gentleman the courtesy of hearing his story before I decide. After that maybe you and I can talk a little about Lucky Luciano."

Sal had wanted to hear the story immediately, but to his chagrin an irresistible force and an immovable object intervened. The irresistible force was Camden; she had joined them toward the end of the conversation, and while not opposed to legends and quests, and truly fond of Charles Moriarty, she was the practical one in this ownership team, and liked seeing the store make enough to stay open even more. She had no intention of crawling back to England defeated, and made this very clear to Sal.

"You cannot just take off in the middle of the day," she informs Sal when he tells her he is leaving to talk with Charles. "We have customers to serve, inventory to log, basically a business to run, remember? And I'm sure Mr. Moriarty needs to get back to his own store for the same reasons."

Charles nods in agreement, then throws up the immovable object just in case Sal had designs on ignoring his cousin.

"I don't feel comfortable talking about this just anywhere," he says, his tone serious. "I don't mind telling you the story, but I don't want just any passerby to overhear the details. Perhaps you could all come to my house for a late supper tonight after our shops close. It has been a long time since I had guests. My grandson Alex visits occasionally, but most of the time I eat alone."

Sal has no choice but to agree, as do Jacob, Julia, and to his dismay, Camden. They set a time, and Charles and Alex leave. When they are gone he wheels angrily on Camden.

"You don't need me here to do any of that stuff you mentioned," he snarls. "Why are you being such a pain in the ass?"

She stares at him coldly and says, "Alpine Valley." Sal's anger melts away in an instant.

"Too loud?" he asks with a grin.

"And too late," she replies, not grinning.

"What the heck are you two talking about," Julia asks, mystified by this cryptic conversation.

"Well, my dear Jules," Sal says, "since you stayed at your parents' house last night, I found myself alone, unable to sleep, and bored. So I pulled out my bootleg copy of Bruce Springsteen live at the Alpine Valley Music Theatre in 1984. Apparently it disturbed the Limey here."

"You played it full blast," Camden says, "at 3:00 in the morning. I am amazed the police didn't show up."

"Fine music is a benefit of sharing an apartment with me," Sal says happily.

"Why didn't you just ask him to turn it down, Cam?" Julia asks, suppressing a laugh.

"I tried! I beat on his door for 20 minutes but he would not answer."

"I was in the moment," Sal says, as if this excuses everything. "But I apologize for keeping you awake. Next time I'll play the Live in Barcelona CD; it has much better sound quality."

Camden starts to reply, reconsiders, and stalks away.

"Why do you constantly provoke her?" Julia asks.

"Because I can," he says. "It keeps me occupied. Otherwise I might notice that the armored car stops across the street at precisely 10:17 a.m. every day, and that Jim, the ancient driver dozes while Ralph, who is even older, is inside, and that he's there for at least seven minutes every time because he has a crush on Flo, the assistant manager who is older still, and that sometimes he doesn't bother to latch the back door of the van completely, allowing an enterprising young man with a special set of skills to make a personal withdrawal from the armored car undetected. You wouldn't want me to notice that kind of thing, now would you?"

"No," she says, taken aback by the detail of what he has just said. "I would not. I like you more as a bookseller than a burglar."

"Me too," he says. "Most of the time."

Acknowledgements

Innumerable people play a part in the creation of any novel, whether they realize it or not. The list runs the gamut from 12th grade English teachers to Kevin Smith to every member, past and present, of the E Street Band. To name everyone would make the acknowledgments longer than the book itself. That said, there are a few that cannot be lumped in with a generic thanks:

Thanks to my sister and new editor, Indi Butler...as always, for everything. Tramps like us, and all that.

Thanks to the eagle-eyed Ellen Stevenson for reading the final proof.

And of course, all my love to my daughters, who get mentioned in both the front and the back of this book. As I've said before, it's more than you expected and less than you deserve.

Paul Combs is a writer living in the not always literary state of Texas. His ultimate goal (besides being a roadie for the E Street Band) is to make reading, writing, and books in general as popular in Texas as high school football. It may take a while.

His first novel, *The Last Word,* was published by The Stratford Press in 2014.